When Angels Whisper

"How we spend Christmas is of greater significance than how much we spend for it."

—Amish Proverb

Sugarcreek Amish Mysteries

When Angels Whisper

NANCY MEHL

Sugarcreek Amish Mysteries is a trademark of Guideposts.

Published by Guideposts
100 Reserve Road, Suite E200
Danbury, CT 06810
Guideposts.org

Cover and interior design by Müllerhaus.
Cover illustration by Bob Kayganich at Illustration Online LLC.
Typeset by Aptara, Inc.

ISBN 978-1-961251-18-2 (hardcover)
ISBN 978-1-961251-19-9 (softcover)
ISBN 978-1-957935-87-4 (epub)

Printed and bound in the United States of America

CHAPTER ONE

Rebecca tugged at her mother's coat. "But what will I get for Christmas, Mama? I want that doll I saw in the window at the toy store. And I want some clothes for her. And—"

"Hush, Boo." Cheryl Miller locked her car doors then turned toward the Swiss Miss, her gift shop in Sugarcreek, Ohio. She looked down at her daughter. "I need to check in with Auntie Esther, and then we'll go home and start decorating for Christmas."

"But, Mama—"

Cheryl sighed. There was still almost a week left until Christmas, and Rebecca's recitation of her wish list was increasing in intensity with each passing day. Cheryl had toyed with the idea of telling her she wouldn't get any gifts at all if she asked for one more thing. But that was rather mean, and Cheryl was embarrassed the thought had even entered her mind. Rebecca had reached the age when she realized that Christmas meant you were supposed to get gifts. Before that she'd just loved the lights, the cookies and candy, and of course, the presents. But she hadn't yet understood that all those things were connected to the word *Christmas* and that it happened every year.

She and Levi had explained to Rebecca more than once that the true meaning of Christmas was to celebrate Jesus's birthday.

However, this year it seemed Jesus was taking a back seat to the long list of toys their eldest child wanted. Although Rebecca had an understanding of who Santa Claus was, Cheryl and Levi didn't want to make him the focus of Christmas. They didn't tell her he wasn't real, because they were concerned she might decide it was her job to enlighten the kids in her Sunday school class with news their parents wouldn't appreciate. It was a dilemma that she and Levi weren't sure how to handle.

Cheryl held Rebecca's hand as they approached the attractive cream-colored building with the cornflower-blue shutters and the bright red door. The Swiss Miss. The reason she'd moved to Sugarcreek. Although she ran the gift shop from a distance now, she still loved the building and the treasures inside.

When she opened the door, the warm air and the wonderful aromas surrounded her. Scented candles, homemade cheeses, and fresh baked goods competed for attention, yet somehow they all blended together to create an inviting aroma that coaxed visitors to take their time looking through the enchanting gifts available. The Swiss Miss was always busy at Christmastime because of the unique items, especially the Amish crafts and foods. There were other shops in Sugarcreek that offered similar products, but most of theirs were made in factories, not created by hand. The homemade Amish quilts were the Swiss Miss's most popular offering. Then there were the Amish faceless dolls along with the beautifully crafted aprons, hot pads, dish towels, and tablecloths. The Amish recipe books compiled by some of the best cooks in the county were also big sellers.

For those looking for special treats to serve their families during the holidays, an assortment of pies, cakes, cookies, fudge, and breads waited in the coolers at the rear of the store. These items sold out quickly, especially the unique desserts like buttermilk, custard, or peanut butter pies. There were apple dumplings, fritters, turnovers, and gingerbread houses for those who wanted to take them home for the holidays.

Esther greeted Cheryl and Rebecca as they walked toward the long wooden counter where she stood at the cash register, wrapping up gifts for a woman Cheryl didn't recognize. But that wasn't surprising, because many people traveled to Sugarcreek during the holiday season to buy things they had a hard time finding in the bigger cities.

Cheryl waited to talk to Esther while Rebecca pulled at her hand, trying to wrest it out of her grasp.

"I want a cookie, Mama," she said for the fourth time. A plate of cookies sat on a small table not far from the display of baked goods.

Cheryl glanced at her watch. Almost five. "All right, pick one to take home for your dessert after supper. And get one for your brother too. But just one for each of you. Do you understand?"

Rebecca nodded solemnly. "Yes, Mama. Just one."

Esther smiled as Rebecca hurried toward the cookies. "Where is Matthew?" she asked after her customer left.

"With Levi at church. He's meeting with the pastor about decorating for Christmas. He's helping to get the nativity set up." Cheryl shook her head. "The structure is a little worse for wear, and Levi says he wants to build something new for next year. I would have volunteered to help organize the decorating, but I just couldn't find the time." She sighed. "Taking care of two small children isn't always easy."

"*Ja*, I know this is true, but you and Levi are wonderful parents."

"Thank you, Esther. I really appreciate that." She turned to glance around the store. "Looks like we've sold quite a few things."

"It has been a good day. Except…" Esther looked around before lowering her voice. "There was a man. A poor homeless man. He came into the shop and looked through some of our gifts. I felt like he was watching me. It made me uncomfortable. I do not want to jump to any conclusions, but I worried that he might be waiting for me to look away, so maybe he could steal something. That is terrible, I know. I offered him some cookies and got him a bottle of water. He accepted them and finally left."

"Did you feel threatened?" Cheryl asked.

Esther bit her lip as she considered Cheryl's question. "I do not think so," she said finally. "It just made me a little uncomfortable. But I did not want to think badly of him because he is homeless. The Lord was also homeless, ja?" She tucked a loose strand of hair under her *kapp*. "I do not wish to think ill of this unfortunate man. I feel rather guilty for eyeing him with such suspicion."

"If you ever really suspect someone of criminal activity, call Chief Twitchell. He can send someone over to check things out."

Esther shook her head. "Perhaps this man only needs a touch of *Gott's* love. Calling the police would certainly not bring that result."

Cheryl admired Esther's sweet spirit. The young woman had a kind heart and saw everyone as a person God loved. And she was right. Yet the Bible advised believers to be as shrewd as serpents and as harmless as doves. Esther was certainly more dove than serpent.

Lydia Troyer, Cheryl's other employee, joined them at the counter. Lydia had left the Amish church several years earlier, but she and Esther were still best friends. Her long dark hair was pulled back into a ponytail, and she wore a sweater and jeans with her red Swiss Miss apron.

"Did you tell Cheryl about that man who came by last night?" she asked Esther.

"Oh my," Esther said. "Where is my head?" She reached into her pocket and pulled out a card, which she handed to Cheryl. "This man wants to talk to you about selling the Swiss Miss." She frowned. "You are not planning to sell, are you?"

Cheryl shook her head. "No. Even if I wanted to, I couldn't. The store doesn't belong completely to me. And the store's income helps pay for my aunt's ministry in Papua New Guinea. She's very dedicated to her work there." Cheryl's gaze swung around the room. "Besides, how could I sell this place? I love it."

"I'm happy to hear that," Lydia said. "This man seems very persistent though. You'd better call him, or I think he'll be hounding you soon."

"Okay." Another thing to add to her already full schedule. Great.

Just then a woman looking at their quilts called over to them, asking for help. Lydia hurried off to assist her.

Rebecca returned with two large sugar cookies in her hands. "I picked these, Mama," she said with a smile. "They are very round."

Cheryl laughed. "Those look like good ones. Why don't you wrap them in a napkin to take home? I don't think we want crumbs on the floor."

Rebecca's face fell. "But I really want to eat mine now."

Cheryl sighed. "You know I told you it was for after supper." She turned to Esther. "I think she picked the biggest cookies she could find."

Rebecca walked slowly over to the table and picked up a napkin. She carefully wrapped the cookies and came back. It was obvious she wasn't happy.

"I will have to bake more cookies tonight," Esther said. She hesitated a moment before saying, "The man…the homeless man? I am afraid he took all the cookies on the plate. I did not stop him, because I felt sorry for him. Thankfully, I had more."

"How do you know he's homeless?" Cheryl asked.

"I have seen him before. And some of the other shop owners have mentioned him. He sleeps at different places around town. Kathy at the Honey Bee found him sleeping on her front porch. You know Kathy. She brought him inside and gave him something to eat. She told him that she would contact churches in the area and see if they could help him find a place to stay, but he told her not to bother. He said he had already tried and everyone was full."

Cheryl frowned. "Surely there's some other place. He can't continue to sleep outside. It's getting colder and colder."

"I agree. I made some calls as well, and as the man said, everyone was full."

Cheryl shook her head. She'd ask her church and see if anyone there could help. "If he comes back, please keep an eye on him. I would hate to have to call the police because he took something from the store."

Esther nodded. "I will do so. Part of my job is to make sure the store and its items are safe."

"I appreciate that." Cheryl looked down at Rebecca, who was fidgeting impatiently. Her mind was on eating her sugar cookie, no doubt, and anything else, even a visit with her beloved aunt, was something standing in the way of her goal.

The front door of the shop swung open, and the little bell over the doorframe rang. A group of four women and two men came inside.

"Do you want me to stay and help you?" Cheryl asked Esther.

Esther shook her head. "Lydia and I can take care of things."

"All right." She smiled. "I don't know what I'd do without you, Esther. You're such a blessing."

Esther's cheeks flushed at Cheryl's praise. "I am sure you could find someone else, but I thank you for your kind words. I love working here. You are the one who blesses me."

Not wanting to get into a gentle disagreement about who was the greatest blessing, Cheryl took Rebecca's hand and headed toward the door. She had almost reached it when she noticed something that made her stop.

"Where's that antique bear?" she asked.

A couple in Sugarcreek had loaned the bear to the shop for the holidays. Cheryl had placed it under a small Christmas tree near the front window. The decorations on the tree included several Amish ornaments. Even though the Amish usually didn't have Christmas trees, many in the community loved to make home-made ornaments and decorations. The display featured English and Amish decorations as well as a few gifts. Besides the stuffed bear, there was a quilt, some homemade candles, jars of jelly, and several other Amish-made toys. Even a handcrafted dollhouse.

Cheryl had assured the couple that the bear would be safe. The Swiss Miss had a security system, and the display was right in the line of sight of anyone working behind the counter. At the time, Cheryl had felt that any real concern about theft was unnec-essary. She'd assumed it wasn't a high-value item and wouldn't be a prime target for thieves. She wasn't even certain how much it was worth.

Esther came around the counter and hurried over to where Cheryl stood.

"Did you remove it?" Cheryl asked.

Even before Esther said anything, Cheryl knew from the expression on her face what she was going to say.

"No," she said slowly. She looked up and met Cheryl's eyes. "I am afraid it has been stolen."

Chapter Two

Cheryl went into the office to call the police and report the theft. She asked for Chief Twitchell, but he wasn't there. She was put through to Officer Abel, who took her report but gave her very little hope that they would be able to find an odd item like that.

"It sounds like something only very specific people would be interested in." He paused for a moment. "I'll call around to the shops in town that handle collectible toys. Let them know someone may try to approach them with it." He asked that Cheryl describe the bear, and she did.

"Doesn't sound like something someone would steal," he said.

"I agree. To be honest, I have no idea what it's worth. I hate calling the Fuszes and telling them it's gone."

"I really hope we can find it," he said. "We'll do our best."

"I know you will. Thanks."

Cheryl hung up and went back out to the front. "I talked to the police," she told Esther. "They're going to alert shops in town to watch out for the bear. I'm hoping someone's child picked it up and carried it off. Maybe the parents will realize what happened and return it. I'm going to wait until tomorrow to contact the Fuszes. I don't want to upset them unnecessarily."

"I will certainly pray for its return," Esther said.

Cheryl thanked her and told Rebecca that it was time for them to leave. Once again, she took Rebecca's hand and headed for the door. But before they reached it, it swung open and a tall, rather imposing woman entered. Her hair was piled on top of her head and was clearly bleached. Cheryl decided she was probably at least sixty years old, but she dressed much younger. Her coat was open, and underneath it she wore jeans and a red blouse. Although she tried not to judge her, the storm cloud around the woman made Cheryl's inner alarm bells ring.

"I want to talk to the owner," she said to Esther when she reached the counter. Cheryl was tempted to run for the exit, but she couldn't do that to Esther. She stopped and turned around.

"I'm the owner," she said. "What can I do for you?"

"You can stop stealing my customers," the woman said, her features twisted in anger.

"I—I don't understand. I haven't stolen anyone's customers."

The woman began to tap her red high-heeled shoes on the floor.

"I'm Kasey Keller. I opened Kasey's Kountry Kupboard a month ago. Just in time for Christmas. We have wonderful Amish gifts and foods." She swung her gaze around the shop. "Much better than what you can offer in this small place." She fixated on Lydia, who had just finished helping a customer and stood with her mouth open, listening to the woman's vitriolic tirade. "That girl has been sending my customers here," she said, her voice raised.

A couple of women who had been looking through the cookbooks moved to the back of the shop, obviously trying to hide.

Lydia looked at Cheryl. "I didn't do any such thing. A friend of mine asked where she could find authentic Amish quilts. She'd been to this woman's store, but all they had were machine-stitched quilts. My friend came here because we have what she was looking for." Lydia shrugged. "I guess she told some people at her church, and they started shopping here. I never tried to steal anyone's customers."

"She admits what she did," the woman shouted, pointing her finger at Lydia. "What are you going to do about it?" she asked Cheryl, who was trying to hold on to her temper. Rebecca was grasping her hand tightly and staring at Kasey, her eyes shiny with tears. Scaring her five-year-old daughter wasn't cool, and Cheryl had had enough.

"I don't intend to do anything about it," she said to the irate woman. "I'd like you to leave now. And please don't come back and talk to my staff—or me—like that ever again. It's not our fault that you're trying to sell your commercially made quilts as if they're the real thing."

Kasey's mouth dropped open, and she sputtered as if trying to find the right words. Finally, she croaked out, "You'll be sorry for this." Then she turned and paused for a long moment, studying the Christmas tree display before storming out of the store. She slammed the front door so hard, the bell overhead almost fell off its bracket.

"I-I'm sorry," Lydia said, her voice shaking. "I certainly wasn't trying to cause a problem."

"You didn't do anything wrong," Cheryl said. "Don't take what she said seriously. That woman has issues." She walked over to the counter and leaned close to Esther. "Did you see how she looked at the tree?"

Esther nodded. Her eyebrows knit together as she said, "Do you think she took the bear? Maybe as a way of getting back at you?"

"I don't know," Cheryl said slowly. "I wouldn't think so. Have either of you seen her in here before?"

Esther shook her head. "No, but she could have come in when we were really busy. Perhaps we missed her?"

Lydia hesitated a moment. "I think I saw her about a week ago. And she has three employees. I saw one of them shopping here a couple of days ago. He didn't buy anything. He was just looking around." She frowned. "You know, I don't think that's the first time he's been in here." She turned to Esther. "I pointed him out to you. Didn't you say you'd seen him before?"

"Ja," Esther said, "and he made me a little nervous. He was studying our inventory. Maybe he was just getting ideas for their shop—keeping an eye on the competition. But every time I looked at him, he was staring at me. It was strange."

"Do you know his name?" Cheryl asked.

"I think it's Dallas," Lydia said. "I saw it on his name tag. I only remember because I wondered if his parents named him after the city."

Cheryl sighed. "I don't think I'll mention Kasey or her employees to the police when I talk to them again about the missing bear. We have no proof whatsoever that they took it, and if the police would happen to question her or one of her employees…"

"Today's performance would be nothing compared to her next one," Lydia said.

The women who had concealed themselves by the refrigerated area in the rear of the store came walking slowly toward them. They each had items in their arms they wanted to buy, so Cheryl said goodbye to Esther and Lydia and headed to the front door, determined to actually leave this time.

She tried to put Kasey out of her mind, but the woman troubled her. Judging by her actions just now, the woman seemed capable of doing whatever she could to hurt the Swiss Miss shop's reputation. Could she have sent her employee into the Swiss Miss with an assignment to take something from the shop to use against them somehow? If so, how could Cheryl prove it?

She led Rebecca to the car and got her strapped into her car seat, but the whole time Cheryl was praying that God would show her what she should do next.

CHAPTER THREE

Once in the car, Cheryl decided to run by the church and check on Levi and Matthew. She wanted to tell Levi about the missing toy. She needed his advice, although she wasn't certain he could tell her anything she didn't already know. She had no evidence at all that Kasey was behind the theft—or even that the bear was stolen.

It only took a few minutes to reach Community Bible Church. Cheryl parked the car in the lot to the side of the church, and after promising Rebecca once again she could eat her cookie soon, she took the cookie from her and put it in the glove compartment. Then she led her toward the front entrance of the church.

She was truly disturbed by the missing toy. Although she didn't know how much it was worth, Naomi had told her it was special to the Fuszes. Even if it wasn't worth a lot of money, she still resented anyone thinking they could just help themselves to items in the store. Who had taken it? Could it have been a child who'd picked it up because it was cute? Or maybe the homeless man Esther told her about? Cheryl found that possibility rather unlikely. What could he do with it? And how would he know its value? It didn't look valuable. Just a fuzzy, stuffed bear. If money had gone missing, that might be something else. That would make some sense.

She found Levi looking over the church's nativity pieces. It was true they were a little shabby. The stable was leaning, and the manger was missing a leg. It was only six days until Christmas. Levi would have to try to repair it the best he could. The main structures should have been taken out of storage at the beginning of the month, but Pastor Brotton hadn't been sure it was in good enough shape to use at all. Now that the church's elders had decided to display it, they'd asked Levi to see what he could do to help their nativity make it through one more season.

As they approached Levi, Cheryl noticed a man talking to Pastor Brotton in the church's doorway. They were both watching as Levi worked to stabilize the stable.

"Hi," Cheryl said to Levi. It was then that she noticed the man's shabby clothing and the dirty backpack he wore. Was this the homeless man Esther had mentioned? Her eyes locked on to his backpack. Was the toy bear in there? Even though she couldn't think of a motive for him to have taken it, she couldn't curb her suspicions.

Levi straightened up and smiled at Cheryl and Rebecca. "Matthew is inside playing with the toys in the nursery. April is with him."

April was one of the young women who worked in children's church. Matthew loved her. Cheryl knew he was as happy as a little clam while Levi was busy.

Rebecca pulled away from Cheryl, ran to her father, and wrapped her arms around his legs. "I love you, Daddy," she said. "When are you comin' home?"

Levi smiled at her. "In a little while," he said.

"I got a cookie at Mama's store, but she won't let me eat it."

Levi's eyes twinkled as he looked at Cheryl. "I take it I am not getting the entire story?"

Cheryl laughed. "I would say that's true. I told her she can have it after supper."

Levi patted his daughter's back. "You need to be patient, Rebecca. You will get your cookie soon."

Although she clearly wasn't happy that her father hadn't sided with her, she still clung to him.

"I don't like being patient," she mumbled.

"Sometimes I do not like it either," Levi said with a smile. "But God wants us to be patient."

"Why?" Rebecca asked.

"Because it is good for us to wait for things we want sometimes," Levi said.

"Why?"

Levi sighed. "We will talk about this later, okay? When we get home."

Rebecca made her way back to Cheryl. She looked rather puzzled. Cheryl wondered just how her husband was going to explain the fruits of the Spirit to their five-year-old. That was certain to be a lively discussion.

"So what do you think?" Cheryl asked, gesturing to the shabby structures.

"I will try to do what I can, but it is just so old." He sighed. "I can repair it and touch up the paint. But next year we must have a new stable and a new manger."

Cheryl waited another moment before sharing her news. "I had to make a call to the police. The antique bear that was in our window display is missing."

Levi straightened up and frowned. "The one that belongs to Herschel and Nettie Fusz?" he asked.

Cheryl nodded. "Someone took it, but I can't figure out why. It's not like the thief could sell it for very much. And it wouldn't interest most people."

"Perhaps a child took it."

"That's exactly what I'm thinking. If so, I'm praying the parents figure it out and return it." She shook her head. "It's cold out here. I'm going to take Rebecca inside and call the police department."

Levi frowned. "I thought you said you already called them?"

"I did. I'm just hoping they've found something," Cheryl said. "When will you be finished?"

"I will be home soon. I need my tools and some wood before I can do any repairs. I will return tomorrow and see what can be done." He turned as Pastor Brotton entered the church and the man with the backpack approached. "Cheryl, this is Timothy. He needs a place to stay, and I told him he could bunk in our *dawdy haus* until he finds something permanent. I was certain you would agree."

Cheryl's mouth dropped open. How could Levi invite this man, a total stranger, to stay on their property without talking to her first?

Unwilling to say anything in front of Timothy, Cheryl smiled before taking Rebecca's hand and hurrying into the church.

She was trying hard to not be upset with Levi. She knew his heart was to help people he thought needed it. But it seemed like a careless act. Was he absolutely sure this man was safe? That he was honest?

Trying not to worry, she went downstairs to the children's classrooms and found Matthew having fun with April. When he saw her, his eyes lit up. "Mama, Mama!" he crowed. He picked up a toy and ran to her, his chubby legs almost getting ahead of the rest of him. He was saying something, but although his vocabulary was growing, sometimes, when he talked too quickly, it was hard to understand him.

"I wan' dis a Chwismas," he said.

Cheryl was trying to concentrate on her precious son, but she was still distracted by Levi's news about Timothy. Before she realized what he'd said, April laughed.

"I think he's saying he wants one of those for Christmas," she said.

"I see you've learned to speak toddler," Cheryl said with a smile.

"It's not hard. He's been going on and on about that puppy ever since he took it out of the toy box."

Cheryl took the toy Matthew held up to her. It was a dog wearing a police uniform. "Oh, I know what this is. This is a character from that TV show he loves."

April nodded. "That's it exactly." She smiled at Matthew. "I don't know. Santa may have already loaded his sleigh with all the toys you already asked for."

"Maybe Santa can buy one from a store," Rebecca said.

"It's a pretty popular toy," April said. "I'm not sure even Santa can find one this late. It's only a few days until Christmas."

Matthew's bottom lip began to quiver. Evidently, he was getting the gist of the conversation.

"You never know, Matty," Cheryl said. "Maybe you'll get one. Let's wait before we get upset, okay?"

Matthew tried to smile, but a tear snaked its way down his cheek.

Cheryl nodded at April. "Can you watch them for a moment?" she asked. "I need to make a phone call."

"Mama called the police because someone stole somethin'," Rebecca said solemnly.

April looked questioningly at Cheryl.

"It's just a small toy," she told April. "Only valuable to someone who's into collectibles." She shrugged. "I'm surprised someone took it, but I feel awful, since it was on loan to us. I just want to see if there are any updates."

"I hope you get it back," April said. "I'll watch the kids. Go ahead and make your call."

Cheryl walked down the hall and out of earshot. She called the station and spoke to one of the officers who worked for the department.

"We're doing what we can," he said, "but it's only been a little while since you reported the theft, Mrs. Miller. We'll call you when we have something." He hesitated a moment. "I really wouldn't get your hopes up. A small item like this is very difficult to recover. I know you already spoke to someone here, but I'd like to know if you have any suspects."

Cheryl hesitated for a moment. Should she mention Kasey? Or Timothy, who was a much more likely suspect in her mind? She wanted to, but in her heart she knew that Levi believed they could help the homeless man, so she told the officer that she had no idea who'd taken the toy bear. She shared Esther's thought about a child grabbing it. The officer said that perhaps a responsible parent would find the toy and try to figure out where it had come from.

"I'm sorry," Cheryl said. "I don't mean to hound you. I've worked with the police enough to know you need more time than this. I'm just nervous about it. I don't want to lose something that doesn't even belong to me."

"I understand. But I promise we'll contact you as soon as we have any information. You just need to trust us."

Cheryl thanked him and hung up. She was embarrassed to have called them so soon. She really didn't want to tell the Fuszes that she'd lost their bear. Now she had to deal with seeing Timothy when she got home. She stared down at the carpet for a minute, preparing herself. She was trying her best not to be angry with Levi, but she was still having a hard time dealing with the knowledge that her husband had made a decision like this without talking to her. Up until now they'd tried to make major decisions together. What was he thinking?

CHAPTER FOUR

It was dark by the time Cheryl got home. The days were so much shorter in the winter. Snowflakes danced in the wind like tiny ballerinas as Cheryl parked her car. Her headlights illuminated their frantic ballet.

"Look, Mama," Rebecca said, pointing at the beauty about them.

Cheryl loved seeing the world through her children's eyes. Things that were an inconvenience to an adult could became something full of wonder in the heart of a child. She watched Rebecca, who gazed at the magical display with a smile on her face.

Cheryl waited a few minutes before saying, "We need to get inside, Boo."

"Okay, Mama," Rebecca said. "Can I eat my cookie when we get in the house?"

Although Cheryl had stipulated that Rebecca needed to wait until after dinner, she just couldn't ask her to wait any longer. She'd done such a good job of practicing patience.

"Yes, when we get inside you can eat your cookie."

Rebecca grinned as she unbuckled herself from her car seat. In a moment she was hurrying toward the front door. Cheryl locked the car and followed her. Levi and Matthew weren't back yet. They were probably bringing Timothy with them. She felt nervous about it and wished she'd brought Matthew home with her. However, she knew Levi would take good care of their son.

When they got in the house, Cheryl unwrapped the cookies and gave one to Rebecca. Rebecca carefully put it on the kitchen table then took off her coat and handed it to Cheryl. She climbed up on a chair and sat down, smiling at her cookie.

"Can I have milk with my cookie, Mama?" she asked.

"Yes." Cheryl hung the coat on a hook in the corner and then retrieved a small plate from one of the cabinets. She was amused by Rebecca's reaction to a simple cookie. It was true that she and Levi discouraged too many treats and tried hard to give their children healthy options. But the way Rebecca was acting made it look as if they never gave their children desserts. Were they being too strict?

Cheryl got the milk out of the refrigerator and poured some into a glass. It suddenly occurred to her that Levi might want her to feed Timothy dinner. She'd planned to heat up her homemade chicken soup tonight and serve it with crackers. Was there enough for three adults and two children? She wasn't sure.

She carried the glass of milk over to the table where Rebecca patiently waited, letting the cookie sit until she had the milk. Cheryl knew she had to have both things before she would begin eating.

"How's that?" she asked Rebecca.

"It's *very* good Mama, *danki*."

Cheryl loved hearing Rebecca use words she'd learned from her Amish grandparents. It was so precious.

She stared up at her mother. Then her little hands broke the large cookie in two. Rebecca held one half out to Cheryl. "For you, Mama."

"Oh, Boo," she said, "that's sweet of you, but I need to get dinner going. Why don't you eat my half this time? Next time I'll be happy to share your cookie."

Without saying another word, Rebecca bit into her cookie and followed it with a big gulp of milk.

Cheryl went to the refrigerator and took out the container of soup. Her daughter's unselfish urge to share her cookie made her wonder if her attitude toward Timothy needed to change. Was she being selfish? Holding on to her cookie? Unwilling to share? Or was she just nervous about bringing someone they didn't know into their home? Levi was usually so careful with his family's safety. He must have seen something in Timothy that made him believe the young homeless man wasn't dangerous.

Cheryl poured the soup into a large pot on the stove. There was more than she'd remembered. She sighed and began removing bowls from the cabinet. She had a choice to make. She could react one of two ways to Levi's decision to welcome a stranger. She could receive him with compassion or with suspicion. And she could be upset with Levi, or she could trust him.

It would certainly take some effort on her part. She still wanted to ask Levi why he hadn't spoken to her before extending an invitation, which she felt justified in doing. But would it help? She suddenly felt something rise up inside her. She really did trust her husband. He'd never let her down. Never put her and the children in danger—and down deep inside she knew he never would. Maybe he was convinced that she knew him well enough to realize that if he'd decided to help Timothy, it was only after he'd considered whether or not it was safe for his family.

"Mama, you're smiling," Rebecca said. "That makes me happy."

Cheryl turned to look at her daughter. "It makes me happy too." She noticed the cookie crumbs on Rebecca's face. "Let's get you cleaned up before Daddy and Matty get home."

She got a damp paper towel and wiped off Rebecca's face. She'd just finished when she heard the truck pull up outside. She carried the plate over to the sink and took a deep breath, trying to prepare herself for the evening ahead. She wanted to stay true to the decision she'd made and to show compassion to Timothy. She whispered a quick prayer.

"God, help me to reach out to this young man. And show us what You would have us do to help him. And thank You for trusting us enough to bring Timothy to us."

She checked on the soup and turned the heat down underneath it. She heard footsteps on the porch and waited for the door to open. She was surprised when only Levi and Matthew came inside. Levi pulled the door closed behind him.

"Where's Timothy?" Cheryl asked.

"I bought him something to eat on the way home," Levi said. "I came to get the key to the dawdy haus." He looked down for a moment then back up at Cheryl. "I am sorry I did not talk to you first about bringing Timothy here. I felt I had to do something. It is so cold. Tonight the temperature will drop to single digits. The churches and shelters in town who help the homeless are all full. I checked before extending an offer. How could I not give him a warm place to sleep when I knew it was in my power? Are you upset with me?"

Cheryl walked over to where Levi stood and wrapped her arms around him. "At first I was," she said softly, "but then I realized that you would never do anything that would threaten our safety. I trust your decision."

Levi hugged her and then stepped back and studied her. "Are you completely sure?"

"I'm sure." She gestured toward the pot of soup on the stove. "I've got plenty of soup. Are you certain you don't want to invite him inside?"

Levi nodded. "Timothy needs to bathe. We stopped on the way home, and I bought him some new clothes. I think we need to wait a bit before asking him into the house. I want to talk to him a little more, although I believe when you hear his story you will want to help him the way I do. I assume the dawdy haus is prepared?"

"It is," Cheryl said. "It's clean, and there are fresh sheets on the bed and towels in the bathroom. I haven't had time to turn on the heat."

Levi turned to the door. "I will take care of that and be back soon for supper."

"Wait a minute." Cheryl hurried to the linen closet in the hallway and removed a couple of blankets. "Give these to him. He may need them tonight."

"Thank you, Cheryl." Levi held out his arms, and Cheryl gave him the blankets.

"What about breakfast?" she said. "I have some cinnamon rolls that he could heat up in the morning, or he can join us."

"The cinnamon rolls would be great," Levi said. "Is there coffee in the other kitchen?"

Cheryl nodded. "Everything he needs to make coffee is there." She got the tray of cinnamon rolls out of the refrigerator. "There are only three left, but it should be enough for him. They're large."

Levi had her put the tray on top of the blankets. "Thank you. I will return in a few minutes." He turned and headed for the door again. Matthew, who had taken off his coat and hung it on a low peg by the front door, came running up to Cheryl. She bent down and picked up her little boy and hugged him tight.

Levi hesitated a moment before turning back. "Timothy has been in prison, Cheryl. He regrets his past and is trying to change his life. His story is a sad one. He has lost so much. In my spirit I know God is calling him. I want to help him find a new life."

Levi opened the door and then closed it behind him, leaving Cheryl shocked with the news that Timothy had spent time in prison. For what? Her trust in Levi slipped some. Was the compassion that she loved him for overshadowing his caution? Was God really behind this?

CHAPTER FIVE

While Levi was getting Timothy settled, Cheryl finished heating supper. She wasn't very hungry herself, since now her stomach was tight with worry.

Her children were oblivious to the potential trouble Timothy could bring. Of course, they were used to people staying in the dawdy haus, so bringing in this stranger meant nothing to them.

They were excited because Cheryl and Levi had promised them they'd cut down a Christmas tree and put it up after supper. She ladled their soup into bowls and started to take the crackers out of the pantry. At the last minute, she changed her mind and set a loaf of sourdough bread and some butter on the table. The children and Levi loved sourdough bread. Cheryl made it from scratch using the starter Naomi had given her. It made for a loaf of delicious bread. By the time everything was ready, Levi was back. She reminded him about the tree and the trimming. When he finished supper, he went to the basement to get the boxes that held their Christmas decorations.

By the time he returned, Cheryl had cleaned up and was waiting on the children to finish. When they saw their daddy, Rebecca clapped her hands and Matthew laughed with glee.

"Finish your soup, and you can help Daddy find our tree," she told them.

The soup began to disappear so quickly she had to caution her children to slow down and chew every bite.

Once they were done, Rebecca got down from the table and Matthew waved his arms as he waited for Cheryl to help him out of his booster seat. Once he was free, he ran over to where Levi waited with Matthew's coat and hat. Cheryl helped Rebecca with her coat, hat, and scarf. Then both children put on their mittens while Levi and Cheryl bundled themselves against the cold as well. When everyone was ready, Levi opened the door and the four of them hurried to the truck. Levi's saw was already waiting next to the garage. He retrieved it and tossed it in the back of the truck while Cheryl got the children buckled in their seats. Then they headed to the woods near their farm. The land was owned by a friend who had invited them to cut down a tree every year at Christmastime.

As they drove down the road, Cheryl turned and stared at the dawdy haus. The lights were on. The house now had electricity. Whenever someone stayed with them who wasn't comfortable with the modern conveniences, they were able to use the fireplace and the woodstoves placed in strategic locations. There were also several kerosene lamps and heaters available if they were needed. Since Timothy wasn't Amish, he would rely on the central heating Levi had originally added to the house for Cheryl's parents.

Levi turned down the road and followed the tree line until they got close to the tree he'd already selected for this year. Once he stopped, Cheryl got the children out of the car while Levi got his saw. Even though he left the truck lights on to illuminate the area, he still needed his flashlight to lead the way to where their Christmas tree waited.

When they reached it, Levi took his saw to it. Cheryl was grateful that it didn't take long to cut it down. Even though she'd dressed warmly, her face felt like a large ice cube. She was ready to go back to their cozy house.

The children squealed with delight when the tree fell. Levi grabbed the trunk in the middle of the tree and hit it firmly against the ground several times to knock off loose needles and other things they didn't want to bring into the house. Then he loaded the tree into the truck. Matthew and Rebecca gazed at it as if they'd found treasure. Cheryl loved to watch her children react to the world. Many times it reminded her of her own childhood, although her parents always had a fake tree. Still, the magic of Christmas was the same whether the tree was real or not.

When they got back to the house, Levi set the tree into a metal stand. While he worked to tighten the screws just right so the tree would stand straight and tall, Cheryl got the broom and swept up the loose needles. Then she went into the kitchen and prepared hot chocolate for everyone. After adding a dollop of whipped cream with a sprinkling of cinnamon to each drink, she put the cups on a tray and carried it into the living room. Matthew—who always got lukewarm cocoa—had a special cup with a top that made it harder for him to spill. The children laughed with delight at the special treat.

As the children drank their cocoa, Cheryl opened the box of ornaments and decorations.

"Oh, Mama," Rebecca said, her eyes large. "Everything is so sparkly."

Cheryl laughed. "Yes, it is sparkly, isn't it?" She picked up an angel covered with silver sequins. "Nana and Papa gave us this one. Every time I see it, I think about them."

She missed her parents. She'd counted on them being here for Christmas, but her father didn't feel he could leave his congregation during the season of Advent. Her mother had told them they would definitely plan a trip in the spring. At least it was something to look forward to.

Once Levi had the tree the way he wanted it, he went back downstairs for the lights. Cheryl continued to take the ornaments out of the box and put them carefully in rows on the coffee table. It took a while, since she had to tell her children the origin of each one. She'd started doing that when Rebecca was old enough to understand, and now it was a Christmas tradition. They both oohed and aahed over each ornament.

Although Levi's parents, Naomi and Seth, didn't put up a tree, they'd made some ornaments for them. Naomi had stitched together some darling felt animals, and Seth had carved an oblong ornament with a wooden horse and buggy inside it. Spots of white paint looked like snow. It was so special. These were incredible treasures that would be passed down in the family.

Levi made his way back upstairs. While he put the lights on the tree, Cheryl lifted a smaller cardboard box from the larger one. It held a nativity her aunt Mitzi had given her years ago.

Cheryl slowly pulled out each piece. Although she knew she'd put the set away carefully last year, she was dismayed to find several of the pieces broken.

"Oh no," she said, tears pricking her eyes.

"What is wrong?" Levi asked.

Cheryl showed him the lamb and one of the wise men broken into a couple of pieces.

"That is not too bad," he said. "I can fix them."

Cheryl reached into the box once again and pulled out another piece. "Oh, Levi," she said, her voice breaking. The baby Jesus was in several pieces.

Levi took the pieces from her. "Oh, Cheryl, I am so sorry. I do not know how this happened." He looked up at her. "I do not think this can be fixed. Perhaps we can find a new one."

Cheryl didn't trust herself to say anything. She just nodded. She couldn't remember a Christmas without this nativity. Was it time to get rid of it? If Levi could fix the other pieces, what about the baby? Would a replacement look right? If it didn't, she wasn't sure she would feel the same about it.

Cheryl got up and went into the kitchen where she placed the pieces that could be repaired into a plastic container. Then she gathered the baby pieces, wrapped them in a paper towel, and reluctantly placed them in the trash, wiping tears from her cheeks. She sighed and tried to remind herself that it was just a possession. Something temporary. It was silly of her to think it would last forever. Hopefully Levi could fix the rest of the nativity. And she would find another baby to fit the manger. It might not be the same, but it would be all right.

Cheryl squared her shoulders and turned to go back into the living room with her family. She was surprised to see Rebecca standing at the door to the kitchen, watching her.

"Don't you want to decorate the tree, Boo?" Cheryl asked her.

"Yeah, but I think I need to feed Mr. Bun Bun first," she said. "He might be hungry."

The family had recently rescued an injured rabbit Levi found. Rebecca promptly named him Mr. Bun Bun, although Cheryl thought the rabbit was female. Rebecca had promised to feed him every day, and Cheryl and Levi had decided it might be a good way to teach her responsibility.

"Okay. Do you want me to go with you?"

Rebecca shook her head. "I can do it by myself."

Cheryl smiled at this. Lately Rebecca had started declaring that she could "do it by myself" for quite a few things. She was capable of doing some of them, but not everything. Although Cheryl loved her independent spirit, there was a voice in her head telling her that someday Rebecca really wouldn't need her the way she did now. Her mother-heart grieved some at the thought, even though she knew it was probably selfish.

Cheryl sighed. "Okay, but get your coat and hat first."

Since the barn wasn't too far from the house, Levi and Cheryl had started allowing Rebecca to go there alone. She was doing a great job taking care of the injured rabbit, and Cheryl was proud of her.

Rebecca turned and went to get her coat. A few minutes later she came back, her stocking cap on her head and her coat buttoned. Unfortunately, she'd gotten the buttons off a bit, and the coat was askew. Cheryl decided not to mention it since it still effectively covered her.

Rebecca went out the door, and Cheryl watched it close behind her, feeling a twinge of worry. Why did she feel that way? Cheryl shook her head. She was probably being overprotective again. Rebecca was fine. Even though the night had started out with Cheryl worrying about Timothy staying in the dawdy haus, it was turning out to be a lovely evening with her family. She returned to the living room and smiled at Levi as he teased Matthew and tried to get him to laugh. He was a wonderful father. Maybe he was a little too compassionate sometimes, but how could she complain about that?

Rebecca waited for Mama to leave the kitchen, and then she snuck back into the house and took the paper towel with the broken baby out of the trash. She was very quiet when she closed the door again so Mama couldn't hear her.

She was walking out to Mr. Bun Bun when she saw big snowflakes in the light that was on the barn. She put her head back and opened her mouth, trying to catch them on her tongue.

When she got to the barn, she tugged on a rope Daddy had added to the latch so she could reach it. When she got inside, she pulled the door shut with another rope.

She said hello to Bun Bun and to their horses, Sampson and the others. She had a hard time with their names so she called them LaLa and Obie. Sampson made a noise when he saw her and put his head down so she could pet his nose. It was so soft.

"I have to take care of Bun Bun now," she said to him after a few good rubs.

Before she got the rabbit's food, she looked around the barn, hoping to find a good hiding place. She walked over to an empty horse stall. She got a plastic pail Daddy used to feed the horses, put it in front of the stall, stood on it, and opened the door. The floor was covered with hay. Rebecca jumped off the bucket and walked to the back of the stall. She pushed some of the hay away from the corner. Then she took the paper towel with the broken pieces of the baby Jesus. She was careful when she put them on the floor and covered them with the hay. Daddy never used this stall, and unless he bought a new horse, it would stay empty for a while.

"There you go," she said to the broken figurine. "You stay here. You'll be safe."

She got up, closed the door to the stall, and put the bucket back. Then she went over to the large pen Daddy had built for Bun Bun.

"How are you doing?" she asked him.

The small bunny slowly hopped over to her. His leg seemed to be doing better, but the way he moved still didn't look right. Daddy had said that they couldn't let him go until his leg was strong. Otherwise, he might not be able to get away from other animals that might want to hurt him.

"I wish you could live with us forever," she told the furry gray bunny. "But my daddy said you wouldn't be happy living in this pen." She sighed. "When you leave, I'll miss you."

Rebecca scooped some of Bun Bun's food from the bucket beside the pen, unlatched his door, and poured the pellets into his bowl. After closing the door, she put her fingers through the side of the pen and stroked Bun Bun's fur. It was soft, just like Sampson's nose. When they first put him in this pen, he didn't like to be petted, but now he seemed to like it more. Especially when it was her. Probably because she gave him food. She didn't care if that was the reason. She liked it.

She needed to get back to the house. If she didn't, Daddy or Mama would come looking for her.

She said goodbye to all the animals, opened the barn door, closed it behind her, and was walking to the house when suddenly something appeared in front of her. It was someone dressed all in white.

Rebecca didn't move. Was this an angel? Her mama had read her stories from the Bible that talked about angels.

"Are you Rebecca?" the angel asked.

She nodded, afraid to speak.

"Please don't tell anyone you saw me. Can you do that for me?"

Again, Rebecca just nodded.

"Thank you." The angel reached into her pocket and took out something small and white. She handed it to Rebecca. "This is for you." She smiled. "I'll see you again soon."

The angel turned and walked toward the trees behind the barn. Rebecca watched her until she disappeared. Then she looked down at the thing the angel had given her. It was made of paper and was in the shape of an angel. She stared at for a little bit, and then she put it into her pocket. The angel told her not to say anything about her. She couldn't let Mama or Daddy see the present the angel gave her.

She started running to the house. As she got close to the door, it suddenly opened. Her mama stood there, looking at the barn. Then she saw Rebecca.

"What took you so long?" she asked.

Rebecca wanted to tell her, but she couldn't. When you made a promise to an angel, you had to keep it. She ran to her mother and grabbed her.

"Are you okay?" Mama asked.

Rebecca tried hard to keep the secret, but it just burst out. "I saw an angel, Mama. A real angel! I'm not supposed to tell you. Will God be mad at me now?"

Chapter Six

Cheryl didn't know what to say. She was fairly certain Rebecca hadn't really come face-to-face with an angel, but what had she seen? Should she and Levi be concerned? She noticed Rebecca looking toward the living room. It was probably the Christmas tree and the ornaments that had made her think of angels.

Levi had finished the lights and had just taken the large angel for the top of the tree out of its box. The wide golden wings and the red velvet dress accented her bisque face. She was beautiful. It was a Christmas decoration passed down from Cheryl's parents. They'd given it to her right after Rebecca was born.

"I promise God's not mad at you, Boo. He loves you. Don't worry about that, okay?"

Rebecca nodded slowly. "Are you sure, Mama?"

"I'm absolutely sure."

Rebecca sniffled several times and then wiped her nose on her sleeve.

"Give me your coat," Cheryl said to her. "We're about ready to put the ornaments on. We'll talk about your angel later, okay?"

Rebecca started to hand her mother her coat, but then she pulled it back. "I can do it."

"Okay."

Cheryl let go of the coat. Rebecca headed toward the hooks while Cheryl returned to where Levi and Matthew waited. Matthew's eyes were huge as he looked at the angel his father held. "Pwetty," he said.

"Rebecca is putting her coat away, and then she'll be right in," Cheryl said. She frowned at Levi. "She said she saw an angel outside."

Levi stopped what he was doing and stared at her. "Do you think someone is out there?"

"I doubt it, but maybe you should take a quick look."

Levi got to his feet and headed for the front door. Cheryl started to tell him to put on his jacket, but he was outside before she had a chance to stop him. She sighed. Levi thought he was indestructible. Although she admired his confidence, the children noticed the things he did and wanted to be just like him. If Daddy could go outside without his coat, why couldn't they? At least Rebecca hadn't noticed. What was taking her so long to put her coat away?

As soon as Cheryl had the thought, Rebecca came into the living room. She pointed at the tree. "Can we put the ornaments on now?"

Cheryl smiled. "As soon as Daddy comes back." She looked over at Matthew, who had taken several ornaments out of the box and was playing with them.

"Matthew!" she said sharply. "Leave those alone. They could break and hurt you." She should have been watching him. Rebecca's "angel" had distracted her.

Matthew's bottom lip began to quiver. Unless Cheryl did something to take his mind off the ornaments, he would probably have a meltdown. She quickly looked through the box and pulled out a wooden cat with arms and legs that went up and down when the attached cord was pulled. She handed it to him.

"You still have to be careful," she said. "Don't pull on the string too hard. You don't want to break him."

His smile confirmed that, at least for a little while, peace would reign in the Miller house.

Rebecca sat down on the couch next to her mother. She was unusually quiet. The past few days she'd been repeating her Christmas list over and over to her parents. Cheryl had expected to hear it tonight, but Rebecca just stared at the tree.

"Rebecca, can you tell me what the angel looked like?"

Rebecca's eyes grew large as she stared at her mother. "Like an angel, Mama."

"Was it a man angel or a lady angel?"

"I think she was a lady angel," Rebecca said.

"Okay." Cheryl felt a little better about this information, but she was still unsettled by the situation. "Do you want more hot chocolate?" she asked.

Rebecca shook her head. "No, thank you."

Cheryl was surprised. Rebecca rarely turned down more hot chocolate.

"Where's Daddy?" Rebecca asked suddenly.

"He went outside. He'll be right back."

"Is he trying to find my angel?"

Rebecca looked so distressed that Cheryl didn't want to tell her the truth, but of course she had to. "Yes, honey. We need to know who's outside our house and why."

"I told you it was an angel. Don't they come to help people? And now Daddy might scare the angel away."

"What did the angel say to you?" Cheryl asked.

Rebecca was quiet for a moment. Then she said, "The angel asked if I was Rebecca. Then she told me not to let anyone know that I saw her." Her eyes grew shiny. "Maybe she won't talk to me anymore because I told."

"I don't think angels act that way, honey," Cheryl said gently. "I don't think angels stop talking to us for something like that."

Rebecca took a big, shuddering breath. "Good," she said, her voice wavering. "I don't want to make an angel mad."

"Did she say anything else?"

Rebecca stared at her mother for a moment then shook her head. "That's all, Mama."

Cheryl got the impression that Rebecca wasn't telling her everything, but at the moment, her mind was focused on something else her little girl had said about the woman she'd encountered. Why would she ask if she was Rebecca? How did she know who she was? Could all of this be Rebecca's imagination, or was someone actually outside their house, watching them? It bothered her that this had happened right after Timothy came to stay. Was it connected? Yet he didn't seem to know anyone in Sugarcreek. If he had, wouldn't he be staying with them? Besides, this woman was near their barn, not the dawdy haus.

"I don't want Daddy to look for the angel," Rebecca said. "Please tell him to come back."

"If it was a real angel, Daddy won't scare her away. Angels aren't afraid of people."

Rebecca studied her for a moment. "You don't believe me do you, Mama?"

"I didn't say that," Cheryl said. "I just said that a real angel won't be afraid of Daddy." She reached over and stroked Rebecca's curly auburn air. "It'll be okay, Boo. Don't worry."

Just then the front door opened and Levi stepped inside. "No one is out there," he said. "The snow has picked up some. If there were any footprints, they're covered up now."

"Do you believe I saw an angel, Daddy?" Rebecca asked.

Levi sat down beside her and wrapped his arms around her. "I believe you think you saw an angel, honey, and I really hope you did. That would be wonderful, wouldn't it?"

Rebecca nodded. "It was awesome, Daddy. She was real. I promise."

"Tell Daddy what the angel said," Cheryl said, her eyes meeting Levi's.

"She knew my name. And she asked me not to tell anyone I saw her." Rebecca's eyes grew shiny. "I shouldn't have told you. She won't come back now."

"If she does come back, I want you to tell Mama or me right away," Levi said to her.

Cheryl could tell he was trying to keep his voice calm even though he was clearly alarmed.

"I have never met an angel, and I really want to," he said with a smile. "Will you do that for me?"

Rebecca looked back and forth at her parents' faces and finally said, "Okay." Her voice trembled slightly, but then she pointed at the ornaments. "Can we please decorate the tree now?"

Levi smiled. "Absolutely. But first I think we all need another treat. How about some brownies?" He grinned at Cheryl, who frowned at him. If their children ate sugar this late, they could be up half the night.

"Just this once?" Levi asked. "I mean, it is Christmas."

Rebecca's eyes lit up. "Oh, Mama," she said, "don't forget Matty's cookie!"

Matthew waved his arms around. "Cookie! Cookie!"

Cheryl couldn't help but laugh. "Okay," she said. "I'll let Matty have his cookie, and you can have a brownie, but you have to eat them first and then wash your hands before we decorate."

"We will, Mama," Rebecca said, the angel drama forgotten.

"And I will wash my hands too," Levi said. "Do I get a brownie?"

Cheryl sighed. "I suppose, although I'm not sure you deserve one."

Levi laughed. "I promise I will try to be more deserving."

"In that case, how can I say no?"

Cheryl got up, gathered the cups, and headed for the kitchen. In the background she could hear Rebecca once again rehearsing the list of the toys she wanted for Christmas. She sighed. Teaching the children what Christmas was really about had turned out to be much harder than they thought it would be.

As she put the brownies and Matthew's cookie on plates, she looked through the kitchen window toward the dawdy haus. The lights were on, and it reminded her that Timothy was out there. A homeless man they didn't know was living on their property, and Rebecca was seeing someone outside that she thought was an angel. What was happening? Could they be in some kind of danger?

CHAPTER SEVEN

Cheryl lay in bed next to Levi. She was wide awake, unable to fall asleep. She heaved a sigh.

Levi turned over to face her. "What is wrong?" he asked. "It has been a busy day. You should be sleeping."

She flipped over and looked at him. "I know you're trying to help Timothy," she said, "but he's a stranger, Levi. We don't really know him. What if he's dangerous? What if he's a thief or something?"

By the glow of the night-light, Cheryl could see his troubled expression.

"I thought you were all right with this," he said. "You told me you trusted my decision. Has that changed because of Rebecca's so-called angel?"

"I do trust you, Levi, but no one is perfect, not even you. To be honest, I don't think I was really okay with Timothy being here, but I knew how much it meant to you." She sighed again. "I'm sorry. This isn't fair to you, since I told you it was fine to bring Timothy home. I guess you could be right. Knowing Rebecca saw someone outside worries me. It's probably why I'm having second thoughts about Timothy. Who could have been out there, Levi?"

"Probably no one. It is Christmas. It could have been the light from the barn shining on a tree. Rebecca is a small child with a vivid imagination. I would not take it so seriously."

"You honestly believe that a light illuminating a tree told Rebecca not to tell us she spoke to it?" She reached over and put her hand on Levi's shoulder. "I think it's possible someone is out there, Levi. We have to be careful, for the sake of the children."

Levi was quiet for a moment before saying, "I do not believe that there is any danger. I have not told you Timothy's story. I wanted him to share it, but I see that we are not going to get any sleep until I set your mind at ease."

"I'm not sure that's possible," Cheryl said. "You said he's been in prison. How can I relax knowing that?"

"Things happen to people, Cheryl. Sometimes a situation is not as it seems."

Cheryl fought back frustration. "I have no idea what that means. If a person is in prison, it means they are a criminal."

"Timothy's parents were drug addicts who died from tainted heroin when he was only thirteen. Timothy's ten-year-old sister went to live with their aunt, but she didn't want to take in two children since she already had three. So Timothy moved in with his grandfather, who took very good care of him. Timothy adored him. As he got older, the grandfather developed early onset Alzheimer's. The disease developed slowly, and the grandfather was very defensive about it, unwilling to accept help. Timothy started taking care of things—like the shopping, a lot of the cooking, and cleaning. He had to do these things in a way so as not to offend his grandfather. He did not want to hurt his pride."

"That's a lot to lay on a teenager," Cheryl said. "What if the grandfather burned down the house? Timothy should have asked for help."

"That is easy for us to say, but what would happen to him if it was decided that his grandfather could no longer care for him? Timothy was afraid his grandfather would end up in a nursing home and he would be put in foster care. That fear drove him to try to hold everything together on his own." Levi shook his head. "But as you probably know by now, it went wrong."

"What happened?"

"Timothy tried to stop his grandfather from driving, but the old man would not allow it. Perhaps it was too hard for him to admit he was losing ground mentally, I do not know. So Timothy insisted that he always accompany his grandfather when he drove. Thankfully, he never went far. Just to the grocery store, the pharmacy, and the church. He knew exactly how to get to all three places, so Timothy felt they were safe until he could finally talk his grandfather into giving up his car."

"That could be really dangerous."

"It is not easy to tell a grown man who has been in charge of his life for many years that he is no longer capable of things he used to do with ease."

"I guess," Cheryl said slowly. She couldn't help but feel sorry for Timothy, even if his choices weren't the best. She couldn't imagine having to tell her father he couldn't drive anymore. He was a strong and independent man who wouldn't take news like that with grace.

Levi took a deep breath and let it out slowly. "One evening the grandfather realized he was out of his blood pressure medicine. He insisted that they go to the pharmacy to get it. Timothy got into the car with him, nervous because his grandfather usually drove during the day. As they turned onto the street toward the pharmacy, Timothy saw a young girl on a bicycle in front of them. He yelled at his grandfather to stop. His grandfather was scared and confused and stepped on the accelerator instead of the brake."

"Oh no," Cheryl said.

"The car hit the girl. Once they were parked, Timothy got out and checked on her. Although she was injured and unconscious, he did not think she was badly hurt. He called for an ambulance and planned to wait for it to arrive. But his grandfather told him they needed to leave. He said if the police realized that he was driving, he would go to prison. Although it was against his better judgment, Timothy told his grandfather that they could leave if he promised to never drive again. The grandfather finally gave in. They returned to their house. But someone had seen the accident and wrote down the license plate number of their car. The police came to the house, found the car, saw the damage, and took them both down to the station."

"I'm not sure I want to hear the rest of this," Cheryl said.

"It is a sad story. The girl died before they could get her to the hospital."

"That's terrible. But I don't understand something. Did Timothy get in trouble because he didn't wait for the ambulance? That was wrong, but surely it wouldn't lead to a long jail sentence. I mean, he wasn't driving, and he was a teenager. It wasn't his fault."

Again, Levi stayed silent for a while. Cheryl was confused. This story was awful, but how could Timothy have gone to prison for this? Then it hit her. "Oh no," she said softly. "Are you saying…"

"Ja," Levi said. "He told the police that he was driving. He could not allow his grandfather to go to prison for what would most probably be the rest of his life. Unfortunately, the grandfather was so afraid that he allowed him to take the blame. Timothy convinced him he would be out soon and that they could go back to their lives. Of course, that did not turn out to be true. Timothy was sentenced to ten years in prison. The grandfather ended up in a nursing home and died about five years later. I guess he told Timothy's aunt the truth, but she did not believe him. She was convinced the Alzheimer's was confusing him. The aunt made it clear to Timothy that she and his sister wanted nothing to do with him."

"Oh, Levi," Cheryl said, compassion overwhelming her heart. "That poor kid."

"Aside from the prison sentence, the girl's family sued Timothy, and he was charged with a large fine. When he was finally free, he tried to find a job, but most employers do not want to hire people who have been in prison. Eventually he found a job at a factory that hired ex-prisoners, but trying to pay the fine took almost every cent he made. He could not pay for a place to live."

"So he gave up and became homeless," Cheryl finished.

"Now you see why I feel we have to help him." Levi flipped over on his back and stared up at the ceiling. "I do not know what the answer is for him, but I do believe God knows how to help him. I want Timothy to know about the God who loves him. Who will never desert him and who has a plan for his life. I cannot walk away from him, Cheryl."

She scooted over and put her head on Levi's chest. "You're wrong," she said. She felt his chest tense. "I just mean that *we* can't walk away from him."

Levi stroked her hair. "Thank you," he whispered.

Before they went to sleep, they prayed for the young man who'd been through so much.

Rebecca could hear her daddy and mama talking softly even though she couldn't hear what they were saying. She waited until it was quiet and then got out of bed, went to her closet, and put her hand in her coat pocket. She took out the gift the angel had given her. It was a little bit smooshed, but she was able to fix it until it looked like it had when the angel gave it to her. She went back to bed and put the paper angel on the pillow next to her. She stared at it until she couldn't stop her sleepy eyes from closing.

CHAPTER EIGHT

Tuesday morning Cheryl got the children up, fed them breakfast, and loaded them into the car. She'd recently joined the church's benevolent committee, and they met every Tuesday morning. She had agreed to fill a role on the committee temporarily in place of a woman who'd recently had a baby, but she was beginning to regret it, not really sure why she'd said yes in the first place. With two young children, her work at home, and a store to oversee, she had more than enough to keep her busy. She probably agreed to it because Pastor Brotton had asked her to do it. She felt honored that he believed she could be an asset.

Because Matthew had suddenly decided that he no longer liked oatmeal, it had taken Cheryl longer than usual to get the children ready. She was running almost ten minutes behind. Although everyone on the committee would understand, she didn't like being late. Once they arrived at the church, she quickly herded Matthew and Rebecca downstairs where the committee members' children were being watched. When she reached the top of the stairs again, she almost ran into an elderly woman who looked lost.

"Do you need help?" Cheryl asked.

"I'm a little bit turned around," the woman said with a timid smile. She had fine, curly white hair smashed down with a black hat that looked as if it was made in the '40s or '50s. She wore a printed dress and a black coat that also looked as if they were designed for someone in a classic black-and-white movie. "I'm looking for Pastor Brotton."

The pastor's office was in the opposite direction from where Cheryl needed to go, but she felt compelled to help her.

"I'll show you where to find him," she said.

"Thank you, dear," the woman said. "My name is Judith Shipman." She held out her age-spotted hand, and Cheryl took it. Judith's skin was soft, and her grip was strong.

"I'm Cheryl Miller," she said as she began heading toward the pastor's office, Judith following behind her. "Are you new to Sugarcreek?"

"Oh, I don't live here. I'm from Arizona. My husband died recently, and my nephew invited me to stay with him for a little while."

"I wonder if I know your nephew," Cheryl said. "What's his name?"

"Jordan Hudson," Judith said. "He hasn't lived here very long."

Cheryl thought for a moment. "I don't recognize his name," she said. "Of course, you never know. I may have met him some-time but just don't remember."

"Maybe." Judith smiled.

"Here we are," Cheryl said, stopping in front of the pastor's office door. She was getting ready to knock when someone called her name. Pastor Brotton was walking toward them.

"Hello, Pastor," Cheryl said. She gestured to the older woman. "This is…"

"Judith?" he said. "I'm sorry I'm running a little late for our meeting."

"As you can see, we're both here at the same time," Judith said. "So neither one of us is really late."

The pastor laughed. "I like the way you think." He opened the door to his office.

"Thank you for your help, Cheryl," Judith said, giving her a smile. "I'm sure we'll see each other again."

Cheryl nodded and scurried away, glancing at her watch and realizing she was now almost fifteen minutes late. She wondered if Judith was wanting to find out more about the church. Maybe that was why she was there to see the pastor. Or maybe she just needed someone to talk to.

Cheryl sighed. She was treating this as if it were a mystery that needed to be solved. Cheryl and Naomi had investigated many mysterious situations together over the years. They both had what Levi had once called "natural nosiness." However, Cheryl and Naomi liked to believe they each had a bit of Sherlock Holmes in their DNA.

Cheryl would be able to discuss everything with Naomi at lunch today. Levi was going to take Matthew and Rebecca so they could get together. It was almost impossible to get a word in edge-wise with the children nearby.

She turned down the hallway where the committee was meeting and jogged to the door, glancing at her watch again. For a second, she considered turning around and heading home, saving herself the embarrassment of walking in late. But she couldn't do that. She had a responsibility. She took a deep breath and opened the door to find the committee members standing around, talking. They hadn't even started yet, and here she was worried everyone would be waiting for her.

"Cheryl!" Maddie Barr, the head of the committee, smiled at her.

"I'm so sorry to be late," Cheryl said breathlessly.

"Nonsense," Maddie said. "Brad was telling us about his new book, and we've been celebrating with him. We were just getting ready to start the meeting. You got here just in time."

Brad McKeehan was a self-published author of spiritual self-help books. Cheryl had nothing against self-published books. Some of her favorite authors had turned to self-publishing and did quite well for themselves. She was always excited when they released a new book. Unfortunately, she felt that Brad's books left a lot to be desired. His advice had little to do with God's grace and power and were centered more on what people could do for themselves. However, his readers seemed to get something out of his books, so maybe she was just missing something.

At that moment, Brad turned her way. "Congratulations," Cheryl said to him, smiling. "What's the name of this one?"

Brad was tall and thin and wore black horn-rimmed glasses low on his nose. "I titled it *Christian, Heal Thyself.*" He smiled back at her. His glasses slipped, and he quickly reached to push them into place.

"Sounds interesting," Cheryl said. "Congratulations again." She turned and walked over to the table set up for their meeting.

She sat down in her usual seat, shrugged off her coat, and put it on the back of the chair. Then she took her notebook and pen from her purse. Her actions seemed to prompt the other five members of the committee to head to the table as well.

Maddie sat at one end while everyone else took seats near her. "Let's start our meeting with prayer," she said. "Cheryl, would you lead us today?"

Cheryl nodded, closed her eyes, and prayed that God would reveal those in their community who needed help and that He would provide the resources to meet those needs. She thanked Him for the committee and for the church, and then she said "Amen."

Several "amens" were heard from the others at the table.

Maddie opened a file that was on the table in front of her. These were request forms filled out by members of the church who needed some kind of assistance. Sometimes there were requests from members for someone in their family or community. And then there were direct requests from people who came to the church looking for help.

Some of the requests could be filled from donations given by church members directly to their outreach. Other times, the pastor or committee members approached people in town who had the ability to provide funds or other kinds of donations. Two months ago, Maddie was able to find a car dealership owner who agreed to offer an automobile to a recent widow with three young children. She needed to get to work, but her car had broken down and couldn't be fixed. The widow was overjoyed when she saw the newer-model vehicle donated by the very generous salesman.

Of course, those kinds of things didn't happen very often. Sometimes the needs that couldn't be met kept Cheryl up at night. She and Levi had stepped in a couple of times to help, but it wasn't something they could do often.

"As you know, we've received several requests from parents who are asking for funds so they can buy their children Christmas gifts," Maddie said. "We sent them a form requesting a list of the things their child wants. I'm going to pass them around, and if you see a family you'd like to provide gifts for, please take that paper for your reference."

Maddie passed the forms around the table. Each committee member glanced over the requests. In the end, none of the forms were returned to her.

"Thank you," Maddie said, smiling at the group. "I knew you all would fill these needs. I would ask that you bring the gifts here by Thursday afternoon. If you could wrap them, that would be great. If you can't, it's okay. We have some volunteers who will be here to wrap and tag them. The parents are supposed to be here Friday morning to pick them up."

She pulled the rest of the papers out of the file then picked up the one on the top. "It seems there's a homeless man in town who needs help. It's already cold, and the rest of the week, temperatures will get to well below freezing. A few of the men in the church went out last night to try to find him, but they weren't successful. If you happen to see him around town, would you call the church? Or you can just call me."

"I know where he is," Cheryl said. "He's staying in our dawdy haus."

There was silence for a moment before Maddie asked, "Is that safe, Cheryl? What do you know about him?"

"Levi has talked to him and feels comfortable about his decision. The man's name is Timothy, and his story is very sad."

Steve Granger, another board member, cleared his throat. "Can we help?" he asked.

"Possibly. He just moved in last night, so I don't know what all we'll need. Right now, we're concentrating on getting him food and keeping him out of the cold."

"Maybe we could buy some groceries," Brad said.

"That would definitely be helpful," Cheryl said. "Levi said he was going to the store today. I can ask him what we might need."

"Sounds good," Maddie said. "Thank you for helping him. I don't think I could have slept tonight if he hadn't been rescued."

Cheryl just nodded. She couldn't take credit for something Levi had done. She felt a sense of pride in her compassionate husband. Maybe someday she would be more like him.

"Would it be possible for you to call Levi now?" Maddie asked. "This is our last meeting for a while. We're taking off after Christmas and won't meet until the middle of January."

"Sure," Cheryl said. She took her phone out of her purse and stepped into the hall. She brought up Levi's cell number and tapped on it. He answered after a few rings.

"Levi, the committee wants to know if they can help Timothy with food. What do you think?"

"Normally, I would say that was a blessing, but I checked on him a little while ago and he had plenty of food."

"I don't understand."

Levi sighed. "I don't either. He wouldn't tell me who gave it to him. According to him the person insisted he keep their identity a secret. All he would say was that..." Levi paused. "You will not believe this, Cheryl. He said it was given to him last night by an angel."

CHAPTER NINE

Cheryl ended the call and went back into the meeting room. The members were discussing the church's upcoming Christmas Eve service. Conversation stopped when she sat down.

"I guess we're fine," Cheryl said. "Someone already gave Timothy a load of groceries. He has plenty right now."

"Who gave it to him?" Brad asked.

"We shouldn't pressure Cheryl and Levi," Maddie said. "Whoever is helping this young man may want to stay anonymous."

"Don't let your left hand know what your right hand is doing," Steve said in a low voice. "I agree with Maddie. Let's leave it alone." He turned his attention to Cheryl. "But if things change, will you let us know?"

"Yes, I will," Cheryl said.

The committee reviewed three more requests. One was for a recent widow in the church. Mamie Abernathy's husband had passed away three months before, leaving her with nothing. Mamie had believed their house was paid off, but after Herbert died, she discovered that he'd taken out a $20,000 loan against the house. The committee didn't have that much in the benevolence fund, so they couldn't pay off the debt. They decided to offer to help her sell her house so she could pay off the loan and assist her in finding a smaller house that would fit her needs. Mamie didn't want to move, but it was possible she didn't have a choice. Steve, who was friends with the president of the bank that held the loan, promised to talk to him to see if he could hold off foreclosure for a while. Knowing the church was going to help her might make the bank a little less nervous.

Another church member, Rosalind Price, had asked for the money to fly to Virginia to see her mother, who was in a nursing home. Her mother had cancer and wasn't expected to live much longer. She wanted to spend her last Christmas with her only child. The cost of the ticket, along with a place for Rosalind to stay, a rental car, and a few other expenses was pretty high. Everything altogether was over two thousand dollars, almost every last penny they had in their fund.

"I don't see any way to do this," Maddie said. "I hate to tell her no. She is such a sweet woman, always trying to help out at the church when she can. She said she can scrape together a few hundred dollars, but she simply doesn't have the rest."

Rosalind worked as a cashier at a local convenience store. She only made minimum wage.

The members looked at each other. It seemed no one had an answer.

"I'll call the company that owns the store where she works and see if they can do anything to help her," Warren Abbot said. Warren was a retired accountant.

"You might also contact an airline to see if they can offer her a lower rate," Brad said.

"Not sure that will work," Warren said. "Besides, it's only five days until Christmas. I doubt there are any open flights."

"Maybe we can pull something off later," Steve said. "After Christmas."

Maddie nodded. "We might have to try that." Her voice cracked at the end of her sentence. "Sorry." She put her hand up to her mouth for a moment. When she took it away her lips trembled. She shook her head. "Six months before she passed away, my mother asked that all the family get together for Christmas. We didn't do it. Told her we'd try the next year. Her death wasn't something we could have foreseen. She fell in her house and hit her head. I've just… I've just always regretted that we didn't fulfill her request." She took a deep, shuddering breath. "Sometimes putting things off for later is a mistake. We need to show our loved ones how much they mean to us when we can."

Cheryl reached over and patted Maddie's arm. "I'm sorry."

Maddie smiled at her. "Thank you."

"Let's all get on the phone and call people in the church," Cheryl said. "See if we can raise the money."

"But what about the plane ticket?" Brad asked. "We can't force an airline to give her a seat to Virginia."

"I guess that's where God comes in," Cheryl said. "We'll have to leave that to Him."

"Okay, one more request," Maddie said. "I think this is something we can do. I believe all of you know Mrs. Perry."

Beverly Perry was a widow who lived a few blocks from the church. She was almost ninety years old. Since she didn't drive anymore, someone usually picked her up and brought her to church on Sunday. Cheryl hadn't seen Mrs. Perry for a while though. She hoped she was all right.

Mrs. Perry had a cat that meant the world to her. She and Grimmy were best friends. When the weather was good, Mrs. Perry would put him in a baby carriage and take him for a short walk. Since it had turned cold they hadn't been out much.

Everyone at the table nodded.

"Grimmy needs surgery. It will cost almost a thousand dollars. And that's with the vet lowering the price." Maddie shook her head. "Grimmy is all Mrs. Perry has. I called the vet and confirmed with her that it's possible the surgery will keep Grimmy going for a few more years." She looked around the table. "What do you all think?"

"Absolutely," Cheryl said. "If Beau was sick I'd do whatever it took to help him."

A couple of other committee members nodded their approval before Brad spoke up.

"I think our funds should go to help people, not animals," he said.

He swung his gaze to Marvin Reddick, a retired teacher who usually followed Brad's leading. "I agree," Marvin said. "It would be nice if we could help take care of every church members' pets. But as Brad said—"

"Wait a minute," Steve interjected. "You're missing the point. This isn't about Grimmy. It's about Mrs. Perry. She lives alone. She needs this companionship. Grimmy keeps her spirits up and stops her from feeling lonely."

"That's right," Maddie said.

"I'm in agreement," Cheryl said. "This is more about Mrs. Perry than Grimmy, although we should care about him too."

"We agreed that we must be unanimous before meeting a need presented to us," Brad said. "Obviously, this need will not be met."

Cheryl realized they were trying to watch out for their funds, but she disagreed. Mrs. Perry needed that cat. "I'll stop by the vet on the way home and see if we can work something out," she said. "Maybe I can find a way to help Grimmy."

She wondered if Pastor Brotton might have some ideas. There were certain church members who were willing to help when someone needed it. Most of the time, they gave the money to the committee. But that didn't mean they wouldn't donate directly to a need like Mrs. Perry's.

"Thanks, Cheryl," Maddie said. "Let me know what you find out. I'm not willing to give up quite yet." She looked around the table. "That's all I have for now. Let's pray, and then we'll adjourn."

Maddie asked Steve to pray. When he finished, Cheryl grabbed her purse and hurried out of the room, not really wanting to talk to anyone. Rather than head down to the children's area, she went straight to the pastor's office. At that moment all she could think about was Beau. What if he needed help and she didn't have the money? Beau wasn't just her cat, he was part of her family. He was all she'd had before she made friends in Sugarcreek and met Levi.

By the time she reached the pastor's office, she had almost talked herself out of talking to him about Grimmy. Maybe she should make an appointment first. After all, he was a busy man.

But before she could turn around and head the other way, his door swung open.

"Are you lurking outside in the hall for a reason?" he asked, the twinkle in his eye making it clear he was joking.

Her indecision must have shown in her expression, because he stepped back and waved her inside.

Cheryl sighed and entered his office, praying she could present Mrs. Perry's need in a way that expressed exactly how she felt.

Chapter Ten

Did you have a good meeting?" Pastor Brotton asked.

Cheryl plopped down in the chair in front of his desk while the pastor took the seat next to her.

"Well, I…" She took a deep breath before starting again. "I guess so. It's just that…"

"Yes?" He frowned. "Is something wrong?"

Cheryl shifted in her chair. She wasn't doing anything inappropriate, was she? Then why was she so uncomfortable?

"I'm concerned about a couple of people," she said finally. "The committee felt we didn't have the resources for their needs, and it's bothering me. I wonder if you might have some suggestions for finding funds outside of the benevolence budget."

The pastor was silent for a moment. Had she said the wrong thing?

Finally, he said, "Actually, some money was recently donated to the church. We may be able to do more than we originally thought."

"Well, that's wonderful news, but that may not solve the problem for at least one situation."

"I'm not sure what you mean."

Cheryl filled him in on Mrs. Perry and Grimmy. "As you know, the committee has to be unanimous when it comes to out-reach requests. Two of our members feel that paying for Grimmy's surgery isn't a good choice for our committee funds."

Pastor Brotton shook his head. "Grimmy is Mrs. Perry's family. She needs him. What's the name of the vet Mrs. Perry uses?"

Cheryl told him, and he nodded.

"Let me take care of this. I'm pretty sure I know someone who might be willing to help outside of the committee funds."

Cheryl smiled. "Oh, thank you, Pastor. I was so worried about this. I was prepared to ask Levi if we could find a way to pay for the surgery. I was going to stop by the vet's office this afternoon and see if she would take payments."

He smiled. "Your compassion is one of the reasons I wanted you on our committee. A couple of the members are very practical, which is important. But I needed some people whose hearts lead them. I certainly have that in you. And in Maddie. She's been such a blessing."

Pastor Brotton stood to his feet but then paused when he noticed that Cheryl didn't follow his lead. "Is there anything else?"

She cleared her throat. "Well, yes. Rosalind Price's mother has cancer, and her mother wants her to fly to Virginia to spend Christmas with her this year since it might be their last chance. You know, Rosalind is her mother's only child."

"That sounds like a good cause. Can't we help her?"

"She needs somewhere around two thousand dollars. And that's if she can even find a flight at this late date."

The pastor was quiet for a moment. "Let me see what I can do about that one as well," he said. "I think this new donation should easily cover it."

Cheryl chuckled. "Do you have some kind of millionaire stashed away that no one knows anything about?"

She expected him to laugh, but he just shrugged. "You never know."

"I sure wish we could help Mrs. Abernathy as well. I realize selling her house and buying something smaller makes sense. But this is really difficult for her. She's lived in that house ever since she and Herbert were married. Over fifty years. Raised her children in that house, rocked her grandchildren and great-grandchildren to sleep in her living room rocker. And if she definitely has to sell, the house needs a lot of improvements if she's going to get a good price for it. So maybe that's something we could help with. We have several contractors and a lot of handymen in our congregation. If the house was fixed up, she could get more money for it."

"The house really does need repairs, and I'm pretty sure some of the contractors in the church would be willing to pitch in. And everyone can paint. Maybe we can put something together like that." He paused for a moment before saying, "You know, her children want her to move into a condo. Something smaller she can take care of."

"Well, either way, whether she decides to stay or to sell, the house needs repairs." Cheryl leaned back in her chair. "I don't suppose you have any miracles lurking in your money stash? Enough to pay off the house *and* fix it up?"

He grinned. "Well, let's just see what happens, okay?"

Cheryl cleared her throat. "You've given me hope that everything will turn out okay for her, for Grimmy, and for Rosalind."

"I'm hoping for the same thing." The pastor got up and walked around to the back of his desk. As he sat down in his chair, he said, "Cheryl, I hear a young man named Timothy is staying in your dawdy haus."

Word sure got around fast in Sugarcreek. "Yes, for now."

"If you and Levi need any help taking care of him, would you let me know? The church could help with food and clothing."

"For now, we're okay, but I appreciate it. If something comes up, I'll let you know. Thank you." She stood. "It sounds like the buildings for the church's yearly nativity are in need of repair."

"Yes, they are. Levi told me he can fix them temporarily so we can get through this year. Next year is a different matter."

"Levi is willing to do whatever needs to be done to get everything in good shape."

Pastor Brotton sighed. "Yeah, he could have done it this year if I'd moved on it faster. Time just got away from me."

"That's completely understandable. How's David doing?"

"He's doing great. Plans to be back in church soon."

Pastor Brotton's son, David, had been in a terrible car accident several months earlier. Pastor and his wife, Angelina, had spent almost all their time at the hospital and then at the rehab center while David recovered. He'd just recently gone home.

"Thanks for your time, Pastor," Cheryl said. "I'd better pick up Rebecca and Matty. I need to get home."

"I'm glad you brought these concerns to me. The church's job is not only to reach out to the community but to also help those in our midst."

"I heard that contributions to the food bank are up," Cheryl said. "And we were able to send over two hundred Bibles to prisoners last month. I feel good about that."

"I do too." He walked to the door and pulled it open. "I'll get back with you soon and let you know how the projects you mentioned are progressing."

"Thank you."

After the door closed behind her, Cheryl hurried downstairs to the children's classrooms. Rebecca and Matthew were the last ones waiting, but another child was just walking down the hallway with his mother. There were several groups meeting in different areas of the church today. Cheryl didn't recognize the mother, but they smiled at each other.

"Mama!" Rebecca called out when she saw Cheryl. "That little girl wants a Baby Plays a Lot for Christmas too. Maybe lots of girls want one. Santa Claus won't run out, will he?"

Mindy, a young woman who regularly volunteered downstairs, smiled ruefully at Cheryl. "I tried to tell her that Santa has lots of Baby Plays a Lots, but I think she needs to hear it from you."

"Oh, Rebecca. I've told you and told you that Santa won't run out. Please quit talking about it."

She noticed Rebecca's bottom lip quivering.

"Look, we need to get home. We'll talk about it more a little later, okay?"

"Okay," she said in a woebegone voice, making Cheryl feel even worse than she already did.

She glanced at Mindy, who smiled at Rebecca. "Don't worry. Everything will be fine."

Matthew ran to his mother and put his arms around her legs. "Mama, Mama. Fishies munch?"

Mindy laughed. "I hate to say it, but I only get about half of what he says."

"Normal for a two-year-old," Cheryl said. "We still don't get all of it either." She nodded at her son. "However, I can tell you that this means he wants fish sticks for lunch."

They both laughed.

"Were they good for you?" Cheryl asked.

Mindy nodded. "They're always good. Rebecca is very excited about Christmas, and I want you to know that she told Sari Loudermilk that if Sari didn't get a Baby Plays a Lot for Christmas, Rebecca would give her the one she gets from Santa Claus. Sari is afraid Santa doesn't have time to get her new address. That's why she's so worried that Santa doesn't have enough."

"What?"

"The Loudermilks are new to the church. They moved here from Indiana. Susan's husband died, so she brought her three children here to live with her sister, Cecilia Grissom. As you can imagine, Susan doesn't have much money. She's meeting with the church's office manager about a job. That's why I was watching the kids for her this morning."

Cheryl knew Cecilia, a widow who lived comfortably but certainly would find it hard to support another adult and three children. She was touched to hear that Rebecca wanted to give away the doll she'd been so obsessed with to a child that might not get one for Christmas. But she wondered just how long that resolve would last.

"One of the other children told everyone she's getting the doll so no one else will get one. That Santa only has one doll. I told the girls that wasn't true, but I'm not sure they believed me."

Cheryl laughed. She understood that most children believed in Santa. She grew up with him. But Levi had been brought up differently, and sometimes all the focus on Santa made her a little uncomfortable. "We'd better get going, Mindy. And thanks for telling me about the Loudermilks. I'm sure some of us would be happy to buy some Christmas gifts for the family. Especially the doll Sari wants."

Mindy smiled. "I was pretty sure you'd say that. That's great news."

Rebecca and Matthew were busy running up and down the hallway. She got them under control and led them outside to the car. She felt weighed down with the needs that had been presented today. How could they meet all of them? It seemed impossible.

She decided to stop by the shop and check in with Esther before lunch. She'd planned to go by the veterinarian's office and talk to her about Grimmy, but now she would wait to see what the pastor could come up with.

She was also worried about the missing antique bear. If it hadn't been returned by today, she'd have to talk to the owners about it. She planned to replace it. She felt guilty about making it so easy to steal. It had just never dawned on her that someone would want an old stuffed bear. Not unless they dealt in antiques and knew its value.

She glanced at her children in the back seat. Rebecca was singing "Itsy Bitsy Spider" for her brother, and Matthew was entranced by it. He loved that song and was trying to sing it along with her. His words sounded quite a bit different than his sister's. Rebecca didn't seem to notice. It was a sweet moment, and it made Cheryl smile.

She checked the time. She was still running late. It seemed to be the theme for the day. After stopping by the Swiss Miss, she would take the children home to be with Levi while she had lunch with Naomi.

Cheryl was really looking forward to seeing Naomi. She felt unsettled in her spirit and needed the love and encouragement her friend and mother-in-law would surely give her.

CHAPTER ELEVEN

Ah, both of the little ones today," Esther said as Cheryl stepped inside the Swiss Miss. Lydia, who was in the back of the shop, came over and smiled at Rebecca and Matthew.

"Would you like to look at the ornaments on our tree?" she asked, winking at Cheryl.

"Yes, please," Rebecca said.

Matthew mimicked his sister's response.

Esther laughed. "They just get cuter all the time."

"We think so," Cheryl said. She lowered her voice. "Did anyone bring the stuffed bear back?"

Esther shook her head. "I am so sorry," she said, "but no."

She leaned over the counter and talked softly so the customers in the store couldn't hear her. "There are other shops that have had items go missing. The music shop is missing CDs, and the clothing store down the street has had several expensive scarves and a couple of purses stolen."

Cheryl frowned. "That's awful, but… I don't know, the bear seems so different. I mean, wouldn't it be difficult to sell? The other items could be resold almost anywhere."

"I think you may be right. Regardless, there is a thief at work in Sugarcreek. We must be observant and make certain we do not become his target again. Lydia and I will do our best to watch over our inventory."

"Thank you, Esther." Cheryl glanced around the store. "It looks like we've sold quite a bit."

"Ja, it has been busy all day." She smiled at Cheryl. "*Maam* says you are having lunch today at Yoder's."

"Yes. I'd better get the children home so I can get there in time to meet her."

"I would take them if we were not so busy." As if on cue, two women walked up to the counter, their arms full of items.

"I appreciate that," Cheryl said, "but Levi is home today. Call me if you need me."

She went over to the Christmas tree, where Lydia was showing Rebecca and Matthew the ornaments. "Thanks for watching them," Cheryl said to her.

"My pleasure." Lydia smiled. "I'd better get back to work. We've been really busy."

As she hurried away, Cheryl took her children's hands and went out the door and to the car, where she strapped them both in. She paused a moment before getting in herself and gazed at the Swiss Miss, remembering when she'd first come to Sugarcreek after a broken engagement, wondering just where she fit in the world. Now, all these years later, she'd met the love of her life, had two children she adored, and found great purpose and satisfaction. She'd learned that no matter how low she felt or how much she doubted that God knew her situation, the truth was, He never stopped caring or loving her.

Cheryl got into the car and drove back to their farm. Levi was in the front yard talking to Timothy. Cheryl parked in the driveway and got the children out.

"I'm running late to meet your mother," she said to Levi when he came over to where she stood. "Can you take the kids now?"

He nodded. "Timothy is going to help me muck out the stalls and feed the horses." He smiled. "As cold as it is getting, this will be a great blessing."

Cheryl had noticed that the temperature seemed to have dropped. "How cold is it supposed to get?"

"Single digits this week. We will need to turn on the heater in the barn during the coldest nights."

Cheryl had worried so much about their beloved horses during particularly cold winters that Levi had installed an insulated forced-air heater on the ceiling of the barn so the horses would stay warm and their water wouldn't freeze when it got especially cold. It was far away from the hay or anything else that could ignite. She knew he had been concerned about them too. Now on the really cold nights, she could sleep soundly, knowing they were warm.

"Are you doing all right in the dawdy haus?" Cheryl asked Timothy.

He smiled shyly. "Thank you, ma'am," he said. "I'm very comfortable."

Timothy was almost unrecognizable as the person Cheryl had first seen. After a shower and putting on clean clothes, it turned out that he was actually a rather nice-looking young man. Since hearing his story, Cheryl really wanted to help him, but she wasn't sure what could be done. Even if he got a job, the fine he owed would have to be paid. Would he just end up homeless again? At least for now, he had a place to stay.

"I need to get back to town," Cheryl said. She hugged Rebecca and Matthew and got going down the road.

It didn't take her long to reach Yoder's Corner. Cheryl found a parking space and hurried inside. Greta Yoder, who owned the restaurant with her husband, August, saw her and came over.

"It has been so long since we have seen you," she exclaimed. "Naomi is already here. I seated her right away so you would not have to wait."

Sure enough, the restaurant was filling up fast. A line was beginning to form near the entrance.

"Thank you, Greta," Cheryl said with a smile. She looked into the dining room and saw Naomi waving at her from a table near the back of the large room.

Cheryl wove her way through the tables, saying hello to several people she knew. In the spring, summer, and fall, Sugarcreek hosted quite a few tourists, but in the winter, the town was mostly filled with those who actually lived there. People drove from nearby towns to buy Christmas gifts but didn't stay long before heading home. Since the weather could be dicey in the winter, tourists who lived far away usually stayed home or ordered online.

As she approached the table where Naomi sat, Cheryl thought again about how much the petite woman wearing a plain blue dress and a white kapp meant to her. Naomi had been her best friend before becoming her mother-in-law. Even though they had differences in the way they practiced their faith, it hadn't hurt their friendship. In fact, it was stronger than ever. At first it was hard for Levi's parents when he left the Amish way of life, but their love for their son—and for Cheryl—helped Naomi and Seth accept them both as treasured family members.

When she reached the table, Cheryl removed her coat and put it on the empty chair next to her. Naomi's thick, black cloak hung over the back of the other chair at the table.

"I am so glad to see you," Naomi said. "It has been too long since we had lunch together." Her brown eyes twinkled with happiness.

Cheryl sighed. "I feel the same way. I've needed this time with you for too long."

As she sat down, Naomi frowned at her. "You look as if you are carrying a heavy burden."

"I'm just tired. There's a lot going on." Actually, having to tell Naomi about the missing bear was bothering her. She'd had no idea it was so obvious.

A waitress came to take their drink orders. After they told her what they wanted, Cheryl decided it was best to get truth off her chest. Until she did, she wouldn't be able to concentrate completely on her friend. But before she could say anything, Naomi raised her hand.

"I know about the bear."

Cheryl stared at Naomi. "I told Esther I wanted to tell you myself." Cheryl had assumed she had time since Esther was living in her own home with her new husband. Obviously, she was wrong.

Naomi smiled. "She did not betray your confidence. Lydia told me when I ran into her this morning."

"I'm so sorry, Naomi. I called the police. I'm hoping that maybe a child picked it up and that the parents will return it." She sighed in frustration. "I'm very confused. Why would anyone steal it? It would be almost impossible to sell. But Officer Abel said he would send word to all the shops in Sugarcreek who might possibly be interested in purchasing an item like it."

"We must pray that Gott will move on the heart of whoever took it and encourage them to return it."

Cheryl nodded in agreement. She still wondered if a child had it, but if that was true, surely his or her parents should have noticed by now and begun to search for the place where they'd picked it up.

"I will talk to the Fuszes and tell them what happened. They are very nice people. I would not worry about it. Besides, perhaps it will still be found."

Cheryl wanted to believe that, but it was difficult. The more time that went by, the more unlikely it was that it would be returned. Maybe Officer Abel would have luck finding it. Of course, most thieves wouldn't try to sell an item in the same town where they stole it.

"I should go with you," Cheryl said. "It's my fault it's gone missing."

Naomi started to reply when a woman walked up to their table. Cheryl looked up and found herself staring into the face of Kasey Keller. The woman's face was twisted in obvious anger.

"So first you steal my customers, and now you actually steal my inventory? I intend to make sure you're arrested for theft!"

Chapter Twelve

Cheryl stared at the woman, open-mouthed. Then she looked around and noticed other customers watching them.

"I have no idea what you're talking about," Cheryl said. Her face felt hot. She was certain she was blushing from embarrassment.

"You're lying. I'll bet you sent that homeless man around town to steal for you. You're probably giving him a place to stay so he'll do what you tell him to."

"Ma'am," Naomi said, "you obviously do not know Cheryl. She would never do something like that. Please walk away from our table. This is not the time or place to talk about something like this. Perhaps you can meet with Cheryl later and discuss the situation."

The woman glared at her. "You can't stop me from saying what I want. And you definitely can't make me leave a public place."

Before Cheryl could say anything else, a man spoke up behind them.

"Maybe they can't," he said. "But I can. This is my business, and I am asking you to leave. You will not talk to my friends like that. Either leave my restaurant or I will call the police."

Cheryl turned in her chair to see August Yoder standing there, his beefy hands on his wide hips. His face was red too, but Cheryl was pretty sure he wasn't embarrassed. He was angry.

Several people sitting near them nodded in agreement. However, Kasey's reaction was much different. She walked up closer to Cheryl, and for a moment Cheryl thought the woman might actually strike her. But instead, she leaned over and spoke quietly.

"You won't get away with this, trust me." Then she turned and walked out of the restaurant.

August came closer to their table. "I am so sorry this happened," he said. "That woman is not welcome here again." He patted Cheryl on the shoulder. "You order anything you want for lunch. It is on us today."

As he walked away, several other people sitting around them voiced their support for Cheryl. Doris Walker, who ran a very successful pastry shop in Sugarcreek, came over to their table. "That woman has been causing trouble all over town. She actually asked me to stop selling whoopie pies because she wanted to sell them in that fake shop of hers."

"Ach, that is unbelievable," Naomi said, expressing the shock that Cheryl felt. How could anyone be that selfish?

"I doubt she'll be in business for long," Doris continued. "First of all, she's ruining her reputation. And second, her merchandise is cheap knockoffs. People around here know what real Amish crafts and food look like." She smiled at Naomi. "Like the things you make."

"Thank you," Naomi said. "That is very kind of you."

"Your jams and jellies are some of my best sellers." Doris straightened up. "Just don't pay any attention to her, Cheryl. She's not worth worrying about."

As Doris walked back to her table, Naomi reached over and patted Cheryl's arm. "Good advice, ja? Just because some people are unhappy, it does not mean we must become like them."

"She's probably been robbed too," Cheryl said, frowning. "Esther said quite a few businesses have been hit."

"You know it always happens around Christmas, but I understand that this time it is much worse."

"Esther was worried about Timothy stealing something," Cheryl said slowly. She explained Timothy's situation to Naomi and then said, "I hope he's not the one behind this. I guess just because he's had a sad past, it doesn't mean he's innocent."

Naomi smiled at her. "And what do you feel inside? Do you believe he is the thief?"

"Do you mean what does my gut tell me?" Cheryl asked, grinning.

Naomi's cheeks turned pink. "Ja, I just cannot bring myself to say that."

Cheryl took a deep breath and let it out. She could feel her body begin to relax just by spending time with Naomi. "You are so good for me. I miss seeing you."

Naomi chuckled. "We were together only a week ago."

"But we used to talk almost every day. I just get so busy with the kids. You know—"

Before she could finish what she wanted to say, the waitress came back to take their order. Cheryl decided on fried sausage and sliced potatoes.

"I planned to have a salad, but now I must change my mind," Naomi said. "I will have the same thing."

Yoder's was famous for their homemade sausage. Although Cheryl tried to eat a mostly nutritious diet, she couldn't turn it down. "I need some comfort food today," she said.

"You must cast your care about the bear," Naomi said quietly. "Herschel and Nettie Fusz are very kind people. They will understand that someone took it. It was not your fault."

"But it really was my fault. When they loaned it to me, I planned to display it in the window. Then, as I was putting up the Christmas tree, I thought of how the bear would look perfect underneath it. But that made it too easy to pick up. It never occurred to me anyone would take something like that. My mistake."

"Ja," Naomi said. "A mistake." She leaned closer to Cheryl. "It has been a while since we had a mystery to solve. Perhaps we can dust off our detective hats and find out who has been stealing things around town."

It was true that the two women had faced many mysteries since they became acquainted. And they had solved most of them. But life—and children—had gotten in the way. Did they really have time to put their heads together again and trap a thief?

The waitress interrupted Cheryl's thoughts as she put their plates on the table in front of them. "August says this is on the house," she said with a smile. "And he insists you also have dessert. If you are too full, we will send it home with you."

Cheryl knew better than to argue with August. He was an incredibly generous and kind man, but he also had a stubborn streak that was familiar to all those who knew him.

"All right," Cheryl said with a sigh. "But I may be taking more than just dessert home. This is too much food." She gestured toward the healthy serving of fried sausage and potatoes on her plate. There was also a plate of the homemade rolls and honey butter that Yoder's was famous for. She and Naomi had picked creamed spinach as their side dish. The waitress left to get it.

"I hope you're prepared to roll me out of here when we're done," Cheryl said.

Naomi was about to answer when a tall man approached their table. He smiled at both of them. "I'm so sorry to bother you, especially after you were accosted so rudely by that woman."

Cheryl didn't know the man. She couldn't remember ever seeing him before. "Can I help you?"

"I'm Richard Crockett. I spoke to one of the women in your store," he said. "So charming. Your store is lovely. Very authentic. Some of the shops I've visited are trying to sell machine-made items as hand-stitched by Amish craftsmen. You all are the real thing."

Cheryl realized who the man was. "You told Esther you were interested in buying the Swiss Miss."

"Yes, that's right." He gestured to the chair next to Cheryl. "Do you mind if I sit down for a moment?"

"I'm sorry, but not only am I not interested in selling, I don't completely own the shop. My aunt is the one who would have to make a decision like that."

"Can I talk to her?"

Cheryl shook her head. "No, I'm sorry. She's currently doing missionary work overseas."

The man hesitated a moment. "Look, at least let me give you a figure to think about. You can let your aunt know what I'm willing to pay for your shop. If the two of you aren't interested, no problem. I promise I won't bother you again." He reached into his pocket, took out a card and pen, and wrote something on the back of the card. He handed it to Cheryl. "I've written a figure down, along with my cell phone number. Like I said, if I don't hear from you, it's okay. I'll just move on. I'm staying at the Carlisle Inn."

Cheryl took the card. This would be the second one. She still hadn't looked at the first. "All right. I'll let my aunt know about your offer."

"Thank you." He started to walk away but then suddenly stopped and turned back. "I noticed a homeless man hanging around your store yesterday. I've been very concerned about him. I wonder if you know what happened to him?"

"He's found a place to stay," Cheryl said. "He's fine. Thanks for caring enough to ask about him."

"She's being modest," Naomi told him. "He is staying in her dawdy haus."

He smiled. "Thank you for your kind heart. I feel so much better. He's been on my mind." He walked back to his table where he appeared to be eating alone.

"He seems like a nice man," Naomi said.

"Yes, he does. I'm glad he's willing to take no for an answer. Aunt Mitzi won't sell the Swiss Miss." Cheryl picked up the card she'd placed on the table. She turned it over, saw the amount the man had written, and almost dropped the card. She held it up for Naomi to see. "This is at least four times what the shop is worth," she said. "Why would he want to throw away so much money?"

"It does not make sense," Naomi agreed. "Unless he does not understand business or property values around here."

Cheryl turned the card over. It seemed Mr. Crockett dealt in real estate. So how could he not know the value of the Swiss Miss? She slid the card into her purse. Of course, she would contact Aunt Mitzi, but it was a waste of time.

She went back to her conversation with Naomi, but she couldn't get Richard Crockett and his exorbitant offer out of her mind.

Chapter Thirteen

Cheryl and Naomi ate lunch slowly while talking about the thefts happening in the downtown shops. Naomi filled Cheryl in on some of the other things that had been stolen. Among the assortment of missing items such as music and purses and scarves, there was a music box with a jeweled tree on the lid from a gift shop's special Christmas exhibit.

"That's kind of similar to the bear. I mean, it was part of a Christmas display," Cheryl said slowly.

"But the music box sounds very decorative," Naomi said. "And the cloth bear is old and certainly not fancy." She paused a moment. "The manager of the cheese store told me that several blocks of very expensive aged cheese went missing from the delicatessen two doors down from them. Perhaps this was for personal consumption, I do not know. Maybe these items were taken so they could be sold somewhere else."

"The thief would have to take them out of town," Cheryl said. "People here would recognize the items." She shook her head. "I don't get it. Something odd is going on here. It's almost as if—"

"This person is stealing just for the sake of stealing?" Naomi finished for her. She frowned. "But why?"

"I have no idea," Cheryl said. "Maybe we're wrong. Could it be that none of these thefts are connected? I mean, are there just more thefts happening this Christmas?"

"I do not think that is the case," Naomi said. "As you know, many of the stores here sell my jams, jellies, and pies. I sell even more at Christmas. Even shops that do not normally sell food know that there is a market for sweet desserts during this time. People like cakes, pies, cookies, and pastries for their holiday celebrations."

"I don't understand," Cheryl said. "What does that have to do—"

"People tell me things when I deliver my goods." She reached down and took a folded sheet of paper from her satchel. She handed it to Cheryl. "Here is a list of the other things that have gone missing from various stores that I do business with."

Cheryl unfolded the paper. There were eight other stores listed. "Does Chief Twitchell know about all of these?"

"I assume he must, but I do not know for certain. Perhaps you could ask him, since you are acquainted with him."

"I...I don't know. I mean, he knows about the bear, but I'm not sure he'd appreciate me asking him about the other thefts. He'd rightly feel that it isn't any of my business."

Naomi shrugged. "Perhaps that is not important. As you can see, the rash of thefts must be connected. There have been robberies in Sugarcreek before, but this is excessive. Unusual."

"You're right about that." Cheryl took a deep breath and let it out. "If a homeless person was taking these things, it would make more sense. I mean, they might be trying to get their hands on anything they could sell for food."

"So you are suspicious of Timothy?"

"No," Cheryl said hesitantly. She met Naomi's eyes and saw doubt there. "No," she said again with more certainty. "Why would he do this? He's safe, warm, and has plenty of food."

"But these items were stolen before he moved in with you, Cheryl."

"I know, but I still can't believe it. I can't believe he's a thief. Levi trusts him, and I trust Levi."

"When people are hungry, they can become quite desperate," Naomi said. "I am not arguing with you. I realize you have great compassion for this young man. But—"

"But I also need to be realistic?"

Naomi smiled at her. "Perhaps."

"Well, I hope you're wrong. Levi would be crushed if he finds out Timothy is a thief—and that he took something from our store."

"I pray this will not happen." Naomi took a bite of her sausage and potatoes. "Ach, this is so good. I make this dish too, but I am afraid August's is better than mine."

"Nonsense," Cheryl said. "Yours is wonderful. You really need to teach me how to make mine better."

"It is such a simple recipe, but August's sausage is the best. Even I do not know how he makes it." She leaned closer to Cheryl. "Do you add garlic to yours?"

Cheryl shook her head. "No, just potatoes, smoked sausage, and onions."

"Try adding garlic. It is the only other thing I put into the pan when I fry sausage."

"Oh brother. I should have thought of that."

"Many cooks do not use garlic with this dish." She chuckled. "Use good smoked sausage and garlic. This will make a difference."

"Thank you, Naomi. I should have asked you about this a long time ago. You've helped me so much with cooking tips and recipes."

"Speaking of food, what do you want me to bring on Sunday?"

"Do you mind making your au gratin potatoes? Another dish I can't cook like you."

"Ja, I will bring them. What else?"

"Buttermilk pie? Do you have time for that?"

Naomi laughed. "Ja, I have time. I already planned it, since you ask for this pie every year."

Cheryl grinned at her. "I guess I do, don't I? Glad you realized that."

Cheryl started to pick up her fork when she suddenly paused and tears came to her eyes.

Naomi looked at her with concern. "Cheryl, what is wrong?"

Cheryl picked up the napkin in her lap and dabbed her eyes. "It's just that I miss our time together. We don't see each other as much as we used to—not only because of the children, but because when we do get together, usually the rest of the family is there too. Time with just the two of us rarely happens anymore."

"You know what," Naomi said suddenly. "You are right. Why don't we plan to get together for lunch once a week from now on. We can plan it for one of the days I am in town delivering my goods to the stores and you are at the Swiss Miss."

Cheryl took a deep breath. "That would make me very happy. I mean…if you truly believe you have the time."

Naomi nodded. "I will *find* the time. This is important."

"Thank you, Naomi. Again, I am sorry for being so lonely for your companionship."

When Naomi looked past her and smiled, Cheryl turned around to see Levi coming toward them. What was he doing here, and where were the children? As he approached, she started to say something, but then she saw the look on his face, and the words froze on her lips. Something was wrong. Was it one of the children? It felt as if her heart had stopped beating for a moment.

Levi sat down in the chair where Cheryl had put her coat, almost knocking it onto the floor.

"Son, what is wrong?" Naomi asked. "And where are the children?"

"Matthew and Rebecca are fine, Cheryl," Levi said. He must have seen her expression and realized that his sudden appearance had frightened her. "They are with Esther at the Swiss Miss. It is Timothy who is in trouble."

"Timothy?" Cheryl's first reaction was relief, but she could tell Levi was really upset. "What's wrong with Timothy?"

"Chief Twitchell received an anonymous call telling him that Timothy has been stealing things from stores in town and that he would find the stolen items hidden in the dawdy haus. We were outside playing with the children when he arrived with one of his officers. Of course, I let them inside the dawdy haus to look around." He took a deep breath. "The chief found the items hidden in the closet, Cheryl. Timothy has been arrested."

CHAPTER FOURTEEN

Cheryl could hardly believe her ears. Timothy was the thief?

"What about the bear?" Naomi asked.

Levi shook his head. "I do not know. He did not tell me everything he found, just that they matched the missing items taken from the stores that reported thefts."

"I don't believe it," Cheryl said, surprised at herself. She was the one who'd been wary of Timothy. Why was she supporting him now?

"I do not want to believe it either," Levi said. "But the evidence…"

"Wait a minute. You and Timothy were outside when the chief arrived? How long had you been out there?"

Levi shrugged. "We were outside working in the barn earlier. Then we went in the house to get lunch for ourselves and the children. We took them back outside to play, and the police came a few minutes later."

Cheryl swung her gaze to Naomi. "Someone could have easily planted the items when they were all in the house having lunch."

"Was the dawdy haus unlocked?" Naomi asked.

"I am sure it was. I had not yet given Timothy a key."

"Then someone could have slipped inside without you seeing them," Cheryl said.

"Ja, I suppose that is possible."

Naomi paused for a moment. "Are you sure he is innocent, Cheryl?"

Cheryl searched her heart. How could she say yes? She didn't know Timothy at all. Levi was the one who'd had so much confidence in him, and now he appeared to be wavering.

"Look," she said, "I may not be completely convinced he didn't do it, but I believe he deserves the benefit of the doubt. Especially with everything he's been through."

Naomi nodded. "If you and Levi believe this, I trust you both."

"So the chief received an anonymous phone call?" Cheryl asked Levi. "During the time you and Timothy were inside? And the dawdy haus was unguarded?" Cheryl leaned back in her chair and crossed her arms. "That's convenient, isn't it?"

"Ach, Cheryl. I know that look," Levi said, smiling for the first time since he'd entered the restaurant. "You and Maam have another mystery to solve, ja?"

"Maybe," Cheryl said. "It looks to me as if someone is framing Timothy. But why? He hasn't been in town very long. It seems like he doesn't know anyone here. So why would anyone want to see him arrested?"

"Good question," Naomi said.

"I need to talk to him, Levi. Let's go to the police station." She gestured to the waitress. When the young woman came to the table, she and Naomi asked for to-go boxes. The waitress wanted to send dessert with them too, but Cheryl told her they'd get some the next time they came for lunch.

A few minutes later they were on their way. Naomi insisted that they drop her off at the Swiss Miss so she could help watch Rebecca and Matthew. Cheryl was relieved. Although Esther would never complain about keeping an eye on them, it was difficult for her to help customers at the same time she attempted to keep two very active children under control.

After leaving Naomi at the shop, Levi and Cheryl drove to the police station. Once inside, they found Delores Delgado, the station's receptionist, sitting at her desk. Her face lit up in a smile. "Cheryl! It's been too long. How are you?" she asked.

"I'm okay," Cheryl said. "How about you?"

"Can't complain." Her smile slipped some. "Is this visit because of Timothy Hicks?"

Hicks? So that was his last name? "Yes, it is. Can we see him, Delores?"

She looked a little unsure of herself, then slowly nodded. "The chief is at lunch. Come with me."

Delores stood and walked to the back of the room. She opened a door, and Cheryl and Levi followed her. They walked down a long hall, passing various offices until they reached the end. Then Delores opened a large door and waved them through. Timothy was sitting on a bench inside a cell, looking down at the floor. His head snapped up when Cheryl and Levi entered, and he looked surprised to see them. Delores closed the door behind them, leaving them alone with Timothy.

"What are you doing here?" he asked.

"We are here because we want to see if you are all right," Levi said.

"I didn't take those things," Timothy said, his voice quivering with emotion. "I don't know how they got into that closet."

"We think someone put them there while you were inside our house with Levi and the children," Cheryl said. "Then they called the chief and told him to look in the dawdy haus for the stolen items."

"Who would do such a thing?" Levi asked. "Is there anyone in town who might want to hurt you? To make you look like a thief?"

"No, no one. I don't even know anyone here."

"Timothy, why did you come here?" Cheryl asked. "If you have no connection to anyone in Sugarcreek?"

"After my grandfather died, I had no one left except a high school friend who wrote to me while I was in prison. He moved here several years ago. He quit writing a couple of years before I got out, but I hoped he might still live in town and that maybe he'd help me." He hung his head. "I know it sounds desperate, but no one else cared about me after I was convicted except Marty. Not even my sister. I never heard from her, or my aunt. They still believe I was the one driving that night."

"So you came here to find Marty," Cheryl said. "What happened?"

"I got here about two weeks ago and went to the return address on his letters, but he wasn't there. The man living in the house told me that Marty died two years ago, about the same time the letters stopped."

Cheryl took a deep breath. It seemed like Timothy couldn't catch a break. "So you just stayed here?"

He shrugged. "I was out of money. There was nowhere else to go."

Cheryl looked at Levi. "Someone is framing Timothy, yet he has no ties to anyone here. It doesn't make sense."

"I'm telling you the truth," Timothy said. "Look, I realize you have no reason to believe me, but I really wish you would. You and Levi tried to help me. No one else has. I want you to know that your trust hasn't been violated. I'm not a thief, and I didn't steal that stuff and hide it in your house."

"The evidence does seem to be stacked against you," Levi said.

"And you are not sure you can have me near your family any longer. I understand."

"Levi, I trust him," Cheryl said. "Please don't—"

Levi put his hand up. "You both are trying to speak for me. Allow me to talk for myself, ja?"

Cheryl nodded, not sure where this was going. Timothy wouldn't meet her eyes.

"I was going to say that even though the evidence says you are guilty, I believe you. We must try to find out who is attempting to make it look as if you are a thief."

Timothy looked up at them, and his eyes filled with tears. "I don't understand how you're able to trust me. I'm not sure I'd do the same thing if I were in your shoes."

Cheryl knew the answer to his confusion, but this didn't feel like the right time to start preaching about grace. That would come. Now she needed to talk to Naomi. They had to try to figure this mystery out, just like they had so many times in the past.

"We will talk to Chief Twitchell and find out how long you will be here," Levi said. "For now, please try not to worry."

"Staying here doesn't bother me," Timothy said. "It's better than being outside in the cold."

"Hopefully, it won't be long," Cheryl said. "Would it be all right if we pray with you before we leave?"

Timothy nodded. "My grandfather used to pray. I miss that."

Levi prayed for Timothy, asking God to protect him and to help them find the truth. Then they said goodbye, and an officer let them out.

"Don't worry about him," he said to Levi and Cheryl. "He'll be fine here."

"Thank you," Cheryl said.

As they walked down the hall, they met the chief coming the other way. "What are you doing here?" he asked. "Are you visiting your friend?"

"Yes," Cheryl said. "Can we talk to you for a second?"

Chief Twitchell opened the door to his office and ushered them inside. He pointed at the two chairs in front of his desk, but they were full of files.

"Sorry," he said, his voice gruff. "Wasn't expectin' company." He grabbed the files and put them on the table behind him. His desk was already full of papers.

Chief Twitchell was tall and skinny, and his posture did not bring to mind a police chief. However, when he opened his mouth, any doubt about his ability to run the police station disappeared.

"We didn't expect to be here either, Chief, but we wanted to talk to you about Timothy."

"You're plannin' on insertin' yourself into an investigation again, aren't you?"

Cheryl and Levi sat down. "Timothy has been staying in our dawdy haus, Chief," Levi said. "He is a nice young man who has fallen on hard times. We do not believe he is guilty of this crime."

"I don't have the luxury of believin' he's innocent just because you think he's a nice young man," the chief said. "He was caught with stolen goods. I have to pay attention to that."

Cheryl shook her head "But—"

"But we get an anonymous call telling us where to find the stuff when Hicks is conveniently out of the house?" He shook his head. "I know you don't believe this, Mrs. Miller, but I wasn't born yesterday. If it looks like a duck and quacks like a duck, it's probably a duck." He pointed at Cheryl. "I can only go by the evidence I have. You know that. You and your Amish friend have gotten into my business more than once, and if you want to help this time, you'd better get busy before I have to transfer Mr. Hicks to the county jail. I'm only supposed to keep him in a holding cell for twenty-four hours. However, it appears I can't get a transport car here until Friday. After that, the county takes over. I can't guarantee anything."

"I understand," Cheryl said. She stood. "We'll do our best."

They started to leave the chief's office when something occurred to Cheryl. She turned back to Chief Twitchell.

"Chief," she said, "that anonymous call you got? How did the person refer to Timothy?"

He frowned at her. "I'm not sure what you mean."

"Did they call him by name?"

Chief Twitchell was quiet for a moment. "Yeah, as a matter of fact, they did. Timothy Hicks."

"Yet until a moment ago we didn't even know his last name," Cheryl said. "Don't you find that suspicious?"

"Yes, ma'am, I do. The person who called knew him. He wasn't just some homeless guy. They knew exactly who he was."

Cheryl nodded. "Was it a man or a woman who called?"

"Delores said she couldn't tell for sure, and she's pretty sharp. They spoke in a forced kinda whisper."

"Thank you, Chief."

As she and Levi left the police station, Cheryl tried to believe she and Naomi could help prove Timothy's innocence. Unfortunately, they didn't have much time to pull something off. Was Timothy about to go through another time of trauma in his life? And was the answer to that question resting directly on her and Naomi's shoulders?

Chapter Fifteen

As they drove to Seth and Naomi's house for supper, Cheryl tried to come up with a suspect who would have a reason to frame Timothy. But her thoughts swirled in circles. Why would anyone in Sugarcreek have a reason to frame him for theft? He claimed that no one here knew him. Yet it was obvious that someone did. She suddenly realized she hadn't asked about the bear. She'd forgotten all about it.

"What was that big sigh for?" Levi asked, looking over at her.

"The bear. I should have asked the chief if it was with the other stolen items."

"You had other things on your mind."

"I realize that, but I owe it to the Fusz family to let them know if the bear has been recovered."

"Call the chief tomorrow and ask him." Levi smiled at her. "I am proud of you, you know."

"For what?"

"For being the kind of person you are. You are a wonderful wife and mother. You run a successful business. But you are also smart and have a talent for figuring out puzzles. You have helped so many people. And now I believe you will find the truth about the robberies in Sugarcreek. Timothy could not have anyone better to help him."

Levi was raised Amish. Praising people wasn't something he did easily. The Amish believed in humility, which meant that they believed in pointing away from people and saving their praise for God. In all the time they'd been together, Levi had rarely been as effusive as he had just been with her.

"Thank you," she said. "That means more than I can say."

Levi glanced over at her and smiled again. Before he could say anything else, Rebecca spoke up from the back seat.

"When will we get to Oma and Opa's house?"

"We're almost there, Boo," Cheryl said.

"I hope Oma makes butterscotch pie. I love it."

Cheryl smiled at her. "Whatever she makes will be delicious," she said. "Remember what we said about being thankful for whatever we are given?"

Rebecca was quiet for a few seconds. Finally, she said, "She might make caramel pie. I would be thankful for that too."

Levi's strangled laughter made it clear he was trying to hold it back. Cheryl shook her head and grinned at him.

"I think that's a good idea," she said.

"Pie! Pie!" Matthew sang out. "Pie! Pie!"

This time Levi and Cheryl both laughed.

"Look, Mama," Rebecca said. "It's the zoo."

The Millers owned a small petting zoo as well as a corn maze. Both were closed for the winter. Rebecca loved the petting zoo, especially the baby goats and the miniature horses. They were all back in the barnyard for now.

Before long they could see the covered bridge that led to the farm. The creek that ran alongside the road was frozen, but when the weather was warm it bubbled and gurgled as it ran between its banks.

Levi turned onto the road and drove through the bridge to the large two-story white house where he'd grown up. They drove past the barn and the corral in front that gave the horses a place to run. Tonight, the arena area was empty. The horses were in the barn where they could stay warm. Seth had given Levi and Cheryl two of their Morgans, Sampson and Obadiah, after Levi and Cheryl were married. They'd purchased Lazarus from a man who'd been abusing him. The name came because they were determined to give him a better life.

Seth had two new Morgans, Jedediah and Zeke, as well as Methuselah, who had been with him a long time. Methuselah didn't do much work anymore, because of his age. Their other horses were for pulling their buggies. Sugar and Spice had been named by Naomi. Cheryl found it funny that the names were so different than what Seth would have chosen.

As they parked the truck, the house door swung open, and light flooded the porch. Even though Seth and Naomi lived without electricity, Cheryl knew the house would be warm and well lit. Between the huge fireplace in the living room and the woodstoves situated strategically around the house, Naomi's house was extremely cozy.

Seth had installed battery-powered lights, phasing out his gas and propane lights because batteries were safer. A small fire had convinced him to make the move, which was approved by the bishop of their local church. Cheryl liked the change. The house was much brighter now than it used to be.

She could hear the Millers' black-and-white collie mix, Rover, barking a welcome to them. Rover had been dumped in the country as a puppy. Seth and Naomi had rescued him, and now he was a valued part of the family.

As they prepared to get out of the car, Cheryl realized that Seth stood on the porch, Rover next to him. "Do you need any help?" he called out.

"No, *Daed*," Levi said loudly. "We are fine."

Once the children were out, they began running toward their opa. They adored Seth, and the feeling was mutual. He squatted down and held out his arms. Rebecca reached him first. Matthew took a little more time making his way up the porch stairs. Levi reached him before he was all the way up and helped him with the final two stairs.

"Opa, Opa," Matthew sang out. Seth's wide smile made it clear that he was as excited to see them as they were to see him. Cheryl was grateful that they were so close. When Levi decided to leave the Amish church and marry Cheryl, there was concern on both sides about their relationship. But love triumphed as they all made the decision to accept each other along with their differences.

Rover, who had so far managed to control himself, began trying to lick the children's faces.

"Puppy! Puppy!" Matthew said, laughing.

"Rover, sit," Seth said. Although it was clearly a struggle to obey, Rover sat.

Seth smiled at him. "Good boy."

"You've done some good work with him, Seth," Cheryl said. "I remember how rambunctious he used to be."

"He just needed some guidance. I guess we all do."

Seth opened the door for them. "It has been too long," he said. "We have missed having you here."

"The children seem to take up a lot of my time," Cheryl said. "Before they were born, when I was working every day, I thought I didn't have much time. Now I wonder what I was thinking."

"I understand," Seth replied. "We know how time-consuming raising children can be."

When they stepped into the large living room with the crackling fire, Cheryl took off her coat and hung it on the coatrack by the door. Before she could remove the children's coats, Elizabeth came into the room.

"Auntie 'Lizbeth," Rebecca said gleefully, running into her outstretched arms.

Imitating his sister, Matthew ran toward them, calling out, "Auntie Isbeth! Auntie Isbeth!"

"I am happy to see you," she said, giving them both a big hug. When they let go, she said, "May I help you remove your coats?"

Both children smiled and nodded. Once their coats were off, Seth took them from Elizabeth and hung them up on the rack with their parents' coats.

Just then Naomi came out of the kitchen, her apron spotted with flour and whatever other ingredients she'd used to make supper. She grinned.

"I would hug you, but I am afraid I would dirty your clothes," she said. "Come on in the kitchen so we can talk while I finish getting everything ready."

"Can I help?" Cheryl asked.

"Perhaps you can fix everyone something to drink?"

"I'd be happy to."

They followed Naomi into the huge kitchen with the long table that could seat a dozen people or even more if everyone crowded together. Seth had made the table himself, and over the years many people had experienced the Millers' hospitality. Cheryl had spent countless hours in this room. The Millers' living room was large and comfortable, but this room was the heart of the house.

Elizabeth helped Rebecca into a chair and then picked Matthew up and put him into the hand-carved wooden highchair that had been used for all six of the Miller children. Three of them, Levi, Caleb, and Sarah, were from Seth's first marriage to Ruth, who died giving birth to Sarah. Esther, Eli, and Elizabeth were Seth and Naomi's children, yet Naomi loved the first three as if they were her very own. They were close to all their children except for Sarah, who had not only walked away from the Amish faith but from her family as well. Cheryl knew Seth and Naomi carried deep hurt in their hearts over Sarah's rejection, but they didn't talk much about it. There was nothing they could do but pray that someday God would heal the breach between them.

As Cheryl gathered the glasses and prepared the drinks, she turned her thoughts to another person who also needed the kind of healing only God could bring. She prayed silently that God would help them find out who wanted Timothy in jail for something he didn't do. She and Naomi didn't have much time, and their mystery-solving skills were rusty. Were they up to this task? For Timothy's sake she prayed that the answer was yes.

CHAPTER SIXTEEN

Dinner was delicious. Naomi's fried chicken was the best Cheryl had ever tasted. She'd tried more than once to follow her mother-in-law's recipe, but she'd never gotten it just right. Naomi seemed to have a secret when it came to her cooking. Her mashed potatoes were fluffy, and her gravy was perfect.

Rebecca had been thrilled to find out that not only had Oma made butterscotch pie, she'd also made caramel pie. She'd talked Levi into allowing her one small piece of each, which delighted Naomi no end.

After supper, Levi and Seth went into the living room. Elizabeth brought out some of the old toys made by her parents for their children when they were younger. Rebecca and Matthew followed her into the living room, where Elizabeth got down on the floor with them. They loved the wooden horse and buggy, the different animals Seth had carefully carved for his children, and the faceless dolls Naomi had stitched together. Matthew particularly loved a train set Seth had made.

Once everyone else was in the living room, Naomi poured two cups of peppermint tea. She handed one to Cheryl then took the other one and sat down at the table.

"Now, what can we do to help Timothy?" she asked.

"I'm not sure, but I'm convinced he didn't rob the stores and hide the loot in the closet. First of all, it's a dumb place to put stolen items. Secondly, what was he going to do with them? None of them could be resold in Sugarcreek. Someone would recognize them. Everyone knows about the thefts. But here's the kicker. Something I found out from Chief Twitchell. The person who called in to the station anonymously? He knew Timothy's name. First and last. Even Levi and I didn't know his last name."

"And Timothy has never lived here before?" Naomi asked.

"No. Never."

"It does not make sense, ain't so?" Naomi said thoughtfully. "So who is behind this?" She sighed. "I cannot remember any puzzle we have tackled with less to go on."

"I agree." Cheryl thought for a moment. "We have to look at newcomers to town. If he doesn't know anyone in Sugarcreek, it might be someone new. Maybe someone who found out he was here."

"But how could that be? If no one here knows Timothy, who would tell someone he was in our town?"

"I don't know," Cheryl said. "I keep trying to wrap my head around this, and I can't come up with anything that will help us."

"I think you are right that we need to look at people new to Sugarcreek, but that may be difficult. I know that very few tourists stay in town at this time of the year, but there are quite a few who travel here to shop for Christmas. Should we consider them?"

"But those people wouldn't have had time to set this up. Nor would they have known about our dawdy haus." Cheryl frowned.

"How long did Timothy say he has been here?" Naomi asked.

"Two weeks."

Cheryl chewed on her lip as she thought. Could she be wrong? Her gut told her she wasn't. "The idea that someone who's lived here a long time has a grudge against Timothy—who just happened to show up in town—is a big stretch. Since we don't have much time, let's just concentrate on people who haven't been here long. At least it's a starting place."

Naomi nodded but didn't say anything. She seemed distracted. Cheryl had noticed it earlier as well.

"Do you disagree with me?" Cheryl asked.

"It is not that," Naomi said. "Something Rebecca told Esther and me today has been bothering me."

"Let me guess. It's about her angel?"

"Ja. What does this mean, Cheryl? I believe in angels, but I find it hard to believe Rebecca met one outside your house who asked her not to tell anyone about the visitation."

"Levi and I feel the same way. We're not sure what really happened. Levi searched our property after Rebecca told us about it but couldn't find anyone out there. We're wondering if she made it up."

"She has not been one to be fanciful," Naomi said, frowning. "Do you think she did?"

Cheryl leaned back in her chair. "I don't know. If she didn't, that means either someone is hanging around outside our house, telling our five-year-old daughter to be quiet about it...or Rebecca saw an angel. I'm not sure which scenario bothers me the most."

Naomi smiled. "I can see your point, although I may have to lean more toward the angel possibility after what I heard this afternoon."

"I don't understand."

"Before you arrived at the restaurant today, Greta Yoder told me something that made my heart rejoice. I was going to tell you at lunch, but that woman yelling at you made me forget."

"What's that?"

"Someone paid off the loan on Mamie Abernathy's house."

Cheryl gasped. "Twenty thousand dollars? Who would do something like that?"

Naomi shrugged. "I do not know, but I would certainly not be wrong in calling them an angel. Whoever it was also gave enough to pay for the repairs the house needs. Now Mamie won't have to move. It is such good news." She paused for a moment and appeared to study Cheryl. "I cannot interpret the look on your face. Is there something that bothers you about this?"

"Well, I'm thrilled, of course. It's just that my pastor said something this morning about someone working on a solution to Mamie's situation. I guess he knew what he was talking about."

"It is such wonderful news. I cannot believe I forgot to mention it sooner."

"Well, Kasey's antics couldn't have helped you remember. Which reminds me. If we're trying to come up with people who haven't been in town long, she would certainly qualify."

"Ja, I think we must put her on the list. But she says someone stole from her as well."

"Sure," Cheryl said after taking a sip of tea. "What better way to make herself look innocent than to claim she's a victim?"

Naomi tapped her fingers on the table for a moment, then she leaned forward and lowered her voice. "I know this sounds judgmental, but I would not put it past that woman. She is…is…hard to love. There, I said it."

Cheryl stared at her mother-in-law for a few seconds before breaking into laughter. Although she tried to keep her look of indignation intact, Naomi also lost the battle and began to laugh.

At that moment, Levi walked into the kitchen. "You two need to hold it down in here. I thought you were working on a solution to Timothy's problem." The twinkle in his eye let Cheryl know he was teasing them.

"We're working on it, we really are," Cheryl said. "I guess we just needed to laugh a little." She grinned at Naomi. "It's your mother's fault."

"I am sure it is," Levi said. "I just came to get Seth and me some coffee."

Naomi stood and got the coffeepot off the stove. Levi took two mugs from the cupboard and set them on the table, and Naomi filled them. Her cheeks were pink with embarrassment. "Now you skedaddle so we can get back to work."

"Here I am, skedaddling," Levi said, smiling at his mother.

When he was gone, Naomi brought the teakettle over and refilled Cheryl's cup. "Now, we must get serious."

"Okay, you're right." Cheryl thought for a moment. "So what about Kasey's employee? Dallas?"

"I do not know who that is," Naomi said.

"Oh, sorry. Esther and Lydia told me about him. Seems he's been hanging around the shop, looking at our inventory but not buying anything. Esther said he makes her uncomfortable."

"Of course, we do not know if he is new in town," Naomi said. "But we could find out. I certainly do not know anyone named Dallas. I would remember that."

"Okay, so tomorrow we'll try to find out more about him."

Naomi got up and fetched a notebook from a drawer. Then she sat down again and began to make notes. "I want to keep track of what we are talking about." When she finished, she looked up again. "Is there anyone else who is new in town?"

"I'm sure there is, but I don't know them," Cheryl said. "Except... No, never mind."

"What were you going to say?"

Cheryl hesitated a moment. "I met an elderly woman at the church this morning. She said she's visiting her nephew who lives here. She was there to talk to Pastor Brotton. I don't know what the meeting was about, but I hardly think she's the kind of person who would be trying to frame someone."

Naomi shrugged. "Perhaps we should consider her though. Age does not mean someone has no anger toward another person."

"I guess you're right."

"Do you remember her name?" Naomi asked.

"Oh dear. What was it?" Cheryl snapped her fingers. "I remember. Judith something."

Naomi wrote the name on her notepad. "We have three names, but there must be other new people in our community."

"This person would have to know that Timothy was staying with us. I think they would also have to be watching the house to see when he would be outside so they could hide the stolen items inside the dawdy haus. It would be rather difficult for someone to have this information and not have some kind of contact with us. How would they know where we live?"

"Perhaps they followed you. Or asked someone about you. Which means that if we find the person they spoke to, it would lead right to the guilty party."

"You're right. It's also likely that we crossed paths with them at some point. And this happened so quickly, Naomi. They had two weeks to come up with their plan and steal those things from the shops. Then they found out Timothy was staying with us, and it only took them a day to plant the stolen items. I think they were under pressure and could have made a mistake. Maybe something that could expose them."

"Ja," Naomi said. "And perhaps they had another plan but changed it once they knew he was staying with you."

"I think you're right," Cheryl said slowly. "They probably intended to put the stolen merchandise somewhere else. But when Timothy moved into the dawdy haus, it gave them the perfect opportunity to carry out their plot. Even if they found out who had taken Timothy in, they couldn't have known where we live, so they would have to ask somebody. But in a town this size, I think whoever they talked to would tell us someone was looking for us."

"I do too," Naomi said. "We look out for each other in Sugar-creek. But…"

Cheryl saw the worried look on Naomi's face. "What's wrong?"

"If this person is trying to hurt Timothy, how do you know they will not also try to hurt the people who are trying to help him? Cheryl, what if your family is in danger?"

Chapter Seventeen

Cheryl understood what Naomi was saying, but she preferred to believe that whoever was behind the robberies in town was focused on Timothy—not on her or her family. Besides, they could have used violence against Timothy when he was living on the streets, and they hadn't. She said as much to Naomi.

"I pray you are right. But please, be careful. Remember that Rebecca may have seen someone loitering around your home. Did you ask her what her 'angel' looked like?"

"I did. She said she looked like an angel. Then she looked at me as if I was crazy."

"Ach, as if her parents should know what angels look like. So this angel was a woman?"

Cheryl nodded. "Yes, but that doesn't make me feel any better. Besides, maybe Rebecca thinks angels are female because so many of them are depicted that way. It could have been a man. Or it may have just been her imagination. I have no idea." She sighed. "You know, children think their parents know everything."

Naomi clasped her hands together. "Sarah did not believe that. She did not think we knew anything." Her eyes grew shiny. "I am sorry. I did not mean to bring her up. I miss her most around Christmastime, I think. She loved Christmas. The decorations. The dinners at church. As you know, we do not celebrate Christmas the same way as *Englischers*, but we did put up colorful trimmings in the house. And we told the story of Christ's birth. She used to love to hear her daed read from the Bible on Christmas Day."

Cheryl reached over and put her hand on Naomi's. "I'm sorry. I still believe someday you'll be reunited with her. She knows about Levi and me. And that we are all close even though Levi goes to a different church. She must know that you would welcome her home."

"I pray that is true. I will never give up hope."

"I noticed you haven't put up any decorations yet."

"It is harder for me now—the longer Sarah stays away. When I look at the ornaments, the garland, and the ribbons around town, I cannot help but think of her. But of course, I will do something for the rest of my children and my grandchildren."

Naomi patted Cheryl's hand, straightened her shoulders, and then pulled her pad closer. She obviously wanted to move on. Cheryl felt deep empathy for her. She'd been praying for years that Sarah would truly make things right with her family. Would that ever happen?

"Is there anyone else we should add to our list?" Naomi asked.

"Well, if we feel strongly that our suspect is someone new in town, I think I'll visit with the chief tomorrow. He would probably know about people who've recently arrived." Cheryl shook her head. "I wish I could check with the hotels in town, but they won't give out information about their customers. And I understand that."

"Talking to the chief is a *goot* idea." Naomi looked up from her list. "I just remembered. What about the man who spoke to you today in the restaurant?"

Cheryl thought for a moment. "You mean the man who wants to buy the Swiss Miss?"

"Ja, I have not seen him before, although I do not know everyone in town. And he specifically asked about Timothy. Do you remember?"

"Yes," Cheryl said slowly. "He wanted to know if Timothy was out of the cold."

Naomi put her hand to her chest. "And I told him he was staying with you." Her eyes went wide. "What was I thinking?"

Cheryl held up her hand. "That's not on you, Naomi. You know how news travels in Sugarcreek. He could have heard that from anyone in town by the end of the day." She shook her head. "But you're right. How could I possibly have forgotten about him?"

"It was because he seemed interested in buying your business. He seemed legitimate. You did not think of him as suspicious. Where is the card he gave you?"

"Actually, I have two of them now. Esther gave me one that he dropped off at the shop. Then there's the one he handed me at the restaurant." She thought for a moment. "I put the first one in my pocket. I'm not wearing the same clothes now. But I think I put the second one in my purse. Hold on, let me get it."

She hurried out of the kitchen and into the living room. Levi and Seth were playing checkers on the coffee table. Elizabeth was playing with Rebecca and Matthew. They laughed as she held up the wooden dolls and pretended they were talking to each other. Cheryl could feel the warmth and love in the room. She sighed with gratitude for the wonderful family she was now a part of.

She found her purse next to one of the wooden rocking chairs and carried it back into the kitchen. Then she sat down at the table and began to search through it. She pulled out her wallet, but the card wasn't in there. After the wallet came a pad of paper and several pens—some of which she couldn't remember owning. She had a bad habit of picking up pens from different places and forgetting to return them. Then there were the two small stuffed animals she carried with her to entertain Matthew when he got fussy. After a bottle of aspirin, hand sanitizer, and a packet of tissues, her fingers clasped over a card.

"Aha," she said. "I found it!"

Naomi laughed. "I have never known a person who carries a purse like yours. It is as if you are trying to bring everything from your house with you."

"I just want to be prepared for every situation," Cheryl said with a grin.

Naomi pointed at the card in Cheryl's hand. "What does it say?"

Cheryl quickly shoved everything else back in her purse and then put it next to her on the floor. She picked up the card she'd set on the tabletop and looked at it.

"I remember his name now. Richard Crockett. He's not a real estate agent though. He's a business broker. There's a telephone number and an address." She looked up at Naomi. "In Akron. I doubt that someone who lives in Akron would be interested in trying to frame Timothy for robberies in Sugarcreek. I imagine he simply wants to buy businesses in Sugarcreek as an investment."

Naomi frowned. "I understand your point, but I still feel his interest in Timothy was somewhat suspicious, don't you?"

Cheryl shrugged. "Not really. I mean, a lot of people in town were concerned and trying to find a way to get Timothy some help. Including the church, right?"

"Ja, you are right."

Cheryl stared at the card for a few seconds. "I guess we shouldn't dismiss him. Even though he doesn't look like a very good suspect, he is someone we don't know, who just showed up in town." She clucked her tongue several times. "I hope we're on the right track."

"I realize that only looking at people who are new to the area seems to limit us, but at this moment, I am not sure we can do anything else. Maybe if we can eliminate these people, then we can move on to other possibilities."

Cheryl agreed. "I guess you're right. But we're running out of time, Naomi. We've got to come up with something quickly. The chief plans to transport Timothy on Friday."

"I believe it would help us to find out the identity of Rebecca's angel. Could this person be our primary suspect?"

"'Our primary suspect'? You haven't been watching CSI in secret, have you?"

Naomi's forehead wrinkled, and she looked confused. "I do not understand. What is a CSI?"

"Never mind," Cheryl said, chuckling. "You're starting to sound like me, you know."

Naomi was silent for a moment and then said, "Danki. I consider that a great compliment."

This time Cheryl didn't laugh. Instead, she had to blink away tears. Maybe it was the Christmas spirit, but she was feeling especially grateful for her friends and her family. Naomi was a gift from God. Maybe they had different beliefs about their faith, but Naomi loved the Lord. And she loved Cheryl. Through her Amish in-laws, Cheryl had learned that their differences mattered less than the love of God that connected His children.

They sat in silence for several seconds. Cheryl was soaking in the warmth of the kitchen, not just from the woodstove but from her beloved friend. Finally, she cleared her throat, trying to gain control over her emotions. "Okay, so tomorrow one of us needs to visit Kasey's store. I'm not sure how we'll do that without her going ballistic again."

"I will take her some samples of my jams and jellies," Naomi said. "While I am there I will try to talk to her employees. Maybe I can learn more about Timothy."

"And I'll go talk to Chief Twitchell. I'll tell him what we're thinking and find out if he has any ideas or knows of any suspicious people in town who might be connected to Timothy in some way. I also intend to tell him Rebecca's story about the angel. What if someone else has mentioned a stranger who has approached their children?"

"Ach, Cheryl. I do not like to even think about something like this in our town."

"Me neither, but he should know."

Naomi nodded. "I agree. I hope the chief does not have a long list of new or suspicious people." She sighed.

"I feel the same way, but he really has a pretty good instinct about these things."

"And what about the broker? Should you check him out a little more?"

"I'll get online when we get home," she said. "If I see anything suspicious, I'll let you know."

"All right. After I go to Kasey's store and you talk to the chief, should we meet?"

"Let's have lunch at the Honey Bee tomorrow. I haven't been there for a long time. I'd love to see Kathy."

Naomi smiled. "Exactly what I was going to suggest."

Just then Levi walked into the kitchen. "The children are tired, Cheryl. Are you and Watson about done?"

Naomi laughed. "How do you know I am Watson? Perhaps I am Sherlock."

Levi smiled at her. "Frankly, I think you are both Sherlocks. But we must get home, Maam. Thank you for the delicious supper."

Naomi got up, went over to Levi, and gave him a kiss on the cheek. "You are most welcome, Son. I wish you would come more often. I confess that I miss you very much."

"We will try," Levi said. "With two little ones..."

"I understand. I have had a few little ones at one time also."

Levi leaned over and kissed his mother's cheek. "I get the message."

Cheryl followed Levi into the living room.

"Ja, your maam is right, Son," Seth said. "If you come over more often, perhaps I would not beat you so badly at checkers. You are certainly out of practice."

Levi laughed. "Ja, this is true."

Seth walked over to Cheryl and held out her coat so she could slide it on. "I am sorry your parents are unable to make it here for Christmas."

"I am too. But we'll still have a wonderful Christmas."

"I do not doubt that."

Seth patted her on the shoulder. He was not a demonstrative man, so the gesture touched Cheryl.

Rebecca and Elizabeth were still playing with the toys, but Cheryl could see Rebecca was getting sleepy. Matthew was already out, lying on the floor, snoring softly.

"He closed his eyes about thirty minutes ago," Elizabeth said.

Levi got the children's coats. Cheryl helped Rebecca with hers while Levi put Matthew's coat and hat on without waking him up. Then he picked him up.

"Rebecca told us the list of toys she wants for Christmas," Elizabeth said. "The list is quite long. She especially desires a certain doll."

Cheryl frowned at her daughter. "Rebecca, I asked you not to talk about that again."

"I know, Mama. But what if Auntie 'Lizbeth and Opa know Santa Claus?" Her expression grew serious.

Levi turned away to hide his face from his daughter while Naomi covered her mouth to keep from laughing. Cheryl felt a little embarrassed. She knew Naomi, Elizabeth, and Seth understood, but Rebecca being so focused on the material things she wanted for Christmas made Cheryl uncomfortable.

They said their goodbyes and went outside. On the way home Cheryl went over the list of suspects she and Naomi had created. Were they on the right track? Or was the guilty person hiding in the shadows? Someone they hadn't considered? She pushed away another question that kept pricking at her mind like an annoying insect. What if Timothy really was guilty? Could she and Naomi be wasting their time, looking for someone who didn't really exist?

CHAPTER EIGHTEEN

The next morning Cheryl got up before everyone else. She enjoyed the quiet as she sat at the kitchen table and sipped her coffee. She would try to talk to Chief Twitchell today. She also planned to go by the toy store not far from the Swiss Miss and buy a Baby Plays a Lot for Rebecca. She and Levi had struggled with the decision. It was important to them that Rebecca learn the real meaning of Christmas, but this particular doll had become her primary focus. They'd considered not getting it as a way to teach her that lesson, but they just couldn't do it.

"It's Christmas," Cheryl had said to Levi. "Maybe this is the wrong way to try to get our point across. Rebecca will be heartbroken if she doesn't get that doll."

Levi frowned at her. "Getting this doll after we have told her time and time again to quit asking… What will this teach her?"

"It will teach her that her method worked even though we told her to stop talking about it," Cheryl said with a sigh. She gazed into his brilliant blue eyes. "But it's Christmas."

He'd stared back at her, the corners of his eyes suddenly crinkling. "Ach, I want to argue the point with you, but I find I cannot. We will get the doll." He smiled and pointed his finger at her. "But next year…"

Cheryl grinned at him and said, "Yeah, next year."

She sighed as she took another sip of her coffee. Being a parent wasn't easy. She was grateful she was going through the experience with Levi. He was always so levelheaded. Well, until he brought Timothy into their lives. This was one time when his compassion may have won over his pragmatism.

Hopefully today she would be able to speak to the chief. He really was a smart man with a good head on his shoulders. He would probably have some insight about who may have tried to frame Timothy for the thefts. That was, if he truly accepted that Timothy might be innocent. His earlier comments made it clear that he was suspicious of the circumstances that led to Timothy's arrest.

Cheryl got up and went to the window. She pulled back the curtain and looked out. It was still dark. Ever since the appearance of Rebecca's "angel," she'd been nervous, wondering if someone may be lurking out there, watching them. It was obviously silly, since it was way too cold for anyone to be outside for very long. But still, it was hard for her to relax completely.

Last night Levi had gone with Rebecca when she went to the barn to feed Bun Bun. He hadn't seen anything that worried him, but he clearly felt the same way she did. They'd decided that for now, it was best not to let their children out of their sight when they were outside.

"What are you doing up so early?" Levi asked as he came into the room. "I felt you get out of bed. Are you all right?"

"I'm fine," Cheryl said. "Just a lot on my mind."

Behind Levi, Beau came strolling into the kitchen, his tail straight up in the air. Cheryl laughed. "I guess you're the main attraction. Once you're up, there's no reason to stay in bed."

"I do not think it's because of any emotional attachment," Levi said wryly. "He knows I am a soft touch and will feed him. You usually get the children's breakfast first and serve His Royal Highness after that. However, he believes I have nothing else to do but think about him."

Cheryl smiled at her husband. He had grown to love Beau, and the cat was crazy about him. Cheryl teased Levi that the cat had bonded with him because Beau had decided that the two guys should stick together.

Beau had certainly been forced to make some adjustments. Before she was married, Cheryl used to take him to the shop every day. Beau seemed to enjoy it there. The customers adored him and gave him a lot of attention. Now, he was here, and although he was obviously content most of the time, for the first couple of years she stayed home after Rebecca was born, he would run to the door every time Cheryl got ready to go somewhere. Beau loved the children, but there were times they were too rough with him.

At that moment, Rebecca walked into the kitchen, rubbing her eyes. "My eyes are awake now."

"Okay, get up in your chair, and I'll fix you some cereal," Cheryl said.

"From the slow cooker?" Rebecca asked.

"No, I'm sorry. Not from the slow cooker this morning."

Rebecca loved the oatmeal Cheryl made with brown sugar, cinnamon, and walnuts. She usually fixed it for breakfast on Wednesday morning, but she'd been so distracted last night, she'd forgotten about it.

"I'll put it in the slow cooker tonight," she said. "It will be ready in the morning."

Rebecca climbed up on her chair. "Okay, Mama. That's all right." She got comfortable in her seat and looked over at Cheryl. "Can I have my special cereal?"

She was referring to a sugary cereal that Cheryl was sorry she'd ever brought into the house. "Not today. But you can have Cheerios."

Rebecca sighed as if this suggestion was akin to twenty lashes. "Can I have a banana with it?"

"Of course, Boo."

Rebecca loved bananas. Since showing her daughter that her favorite fruit could be added to the dreaded unsugary cereal, getting her to eat it was now much easier.

Suddenly, the smell of stinky cat food flooded the room. Although Cheryl rarely noticed it when she was single, now that she shared her home with three other human beings, the aroma seemed even more pungent.

"Matty, we're having cat food for breakfast," Rebecca said as Matthew came into the room.

"No cat foo," he said, beginning to tear up.

"Rebecca!" Cheryl said. "Stop that." She smiled, reassuring her son. "We're not having cat food. You're having cereal."

Matthew sniffled a couple of times. "Okay."

Cheryl helped him into his booster seat and then poured orange juice for the children.

"So are you and Maam meeting for lunch again today?" Levi asked as he poured two bowls of cereal.

"Yes. I'm so sorry to leave you alone with Rebecca and Matty again. I know you have chores around the farm. But I'm sure they'll love trying to help you."

Levi chuckled. "Spending time with my children is not a chore, Cheryl. I enjoy it. Since there are fewer duties in the winter, it is not a problem. I feel you and Maam should meet more often. She has missed your lunches."

"I know. It's just…"

"That you feel guilty leaving me with the children. But if it becomes a problem, I will tell you. They are my children as well, Cheryl. You should be able to do other things sometimes. Besides, I am glad that you and Maam are spending time together. Perhaps something good will come out of this—besides finding out who really stole things from our shops." He studied her for a moment. "What about the antique bear? Was it in the items recovered from the dawdy haus?"

"I'm not sure, but I intend to ask the chief this morning. I certainly hope the police have it. I feel so bad that the Fuszes trusted me to protect it and someone walked off with it."

"They are very nice people. I do not believe they will blame you for something that is someone else's fault."

Cheryl was comforted by Levi's words, yet she still felt she should have taken better precautions.

"You're probably right," she replied. "At least if the chief has it, I can tell the Fuszes that they'll get the bear back at some point." She sighed. "Right now, it's evidence."

As they ate their breakfast, Levi and the children talked and laughed, but Cheryl didn't really hear them. All she could think about was the small stuffed bear, and she hoped today it would finally be recovered.

Chapter Nineteen

Levi went outside after breakfast to take care of the animals. While he was busy, Cheryl cleaned up the kitchen, bathed Matthew and Rebecca, and got them dressed. Then, as they played, she did a load of laundry, cleaned the bathroom, and ran the sweeper. After that she called the police station and was able to make an appointment to meet with the chief.

She'd just changed her clothes when Levi returned. She wanted to ask if he'd seen anyone outside who shouldn't be there, but she was aware that if he had, he would tell her.

She tried not to worry about Rebecca's angel, but at night she found herself lying in bed, jumping at noises, wondering if someone was outside watching the house. Until they found the person Rebecca saw, or determined it was her imagination, Cheryl wasn't sure she would ever be able to sleep soundly again.

Once Levi was ready to watch the children, Cheryl drove to the police station to meet with Chief Twitchell. She'd been afraid of running late, but she actually got there a minute early. The chief didn't appreciate tardiness. Delores greeted her and said, "He's ready, hon. Go on back."

Cheryl went through the door and down the hall to the chief's office. She rapped on the door and heard, "Come in!"

She opened the door and found Chief Twitchell sitting behind his desk, a frown on his face. At least this time there were no files on the chairs in front of his desk. She sat down and smiled at the chief, who seemed to be eyeing her with suspicion.

"I don't suppose the bear has turned up?" Cheryl asked him.

"No. Sorry. You have anything that will help your friend?" he asked gruffly.

Cheryl sighed and shook her head. "Not yet, but we have some suspects."

"I told you I need evidence. I can't do anything with your suspicions."

"I realize that," Cheryl said. "But we need your help."

She quickly explained the conclusions she and Naomi had come to and the people they were looking at. "Since Timothy isn't from around here, and his friend died a couple of years ago, we feel that whoever set him up might be someone new to town."

"Maybe some thief just picked Mr. Hicks because they thought he was a good patsy. I'm not sure your theories add up."

"I understand, Chief, but why wait until after Timothy moves into our place to set him up? It was much more difficult than putting the stuff somewhere else he'd been. It doesn't make sense."

"I realize that. I told you this thing stinks, but you're not bringin' me anything that will help me arrest anyone else."

"I know. But we're trying. I need to ask you something. Besides Kasey Keller and her employee Dallas, there's someone else that worries us." She told him about Rebecca's angel, watching his face to see if he thought she was being ridiculous, but he looked concerned as she told him about it. "Levi and I wonder if the angel could be Rebecca's imagination. Maybe Christmas has put ideas into her head."

He wrote something on his notepad. "We'll keep an eye on your place. Can't do it twenty-four hours, but when my officers are out, I'll have them swing by."

"Thank you. And one other thing. Have you seen any other new people around town who seem suspicious?"

The chief thought for a moment. "You know we don't get a lot of tourists this close to Christmas, just people who can get home in case the weather turns bad. I haven't seen anyone acting unusual, except one guy maybe. Tall guy, dark hair. Wears a suit. Looks out of place. He's been hangin' around downtown for a while."

"That sounds like Richard Crockett." Cheryl leaned over and picked her purse up off the floor. She'd put both of Crockett's cards in her wallet so she would know where they were. She pulled one out and handed it to the chief.

After looking at it, he said, "And why are you talkin' to him? You're not thinkin' about sellin' the Swiss Miss, are you?"

"No. And I'm certain Aunt Mitzi isn't interested either."

"I'm not sure he makes a good suspect. He doesn't live here. Seems like he's just tryin' to find businesses to buy. Sugarcreek is a great place for shops like yours."

"Yeah, I guess so. He offered a lot for it. I actually looked him up online last night and found his website. He seems legitimate."

Chief Twitchell grunted. "A lot of times these brokers offer a high price to get you interested but then whittle the price down before a final offer. It's a way to reel a business owner in and get 'em interested. Once they've baited the hook, the owners are reluctant to walk away. I've seen it before here in Sugarcreek."

"I'm sure you're right. There doesn't seem to be any reason for Mr. Crockett to be interested in Timothy." She sighed. "I was hoping you would have some insight—something to send us in the right direction."

"Well, I still might be able to do that. You mentioned the woman who opened Kasey's Kountry Kupboard a few weeks ago?"

"Yes, her and one of her employees. They've been acting rather odd, and Timothy arrived here before she did."

Chief Twitchell crossed his arms over his chest and leaned back in his chair. "She opened that shop of hers pretty quick. Her stuff is cheap. Nothin' like what shops like yours offer. I found it odd and did some checkin' on her. Seems she bought that empty store sight unseen. For twice what it's worth. She ran a couple of other businesses into the ground in other cities. She's got a rich father who keeps bankrollin' her. He paid off her unpaid taxes and helped her get this place."

"But why would she have it out for Timothy?"

The chief shrugged. "I didn't see a connection between them, but I wasn't really looking."

"Before she left my shop, she lingered at the Christmas tree where I had the antique bear. It seemed odd," Cheryl said. "But that's the only thing about her that made me wonder if she had anything to do with taking it."

"That bear just doesn't fit with the rest of the stolen items," Chief Twitchell said. "That bothers me."

"Me too," Cheryl said. She shook her head. "Chief, are you sure the bear wasn't found with the other items?"

"Nah. No stuffed bear. Just purses, scarves, and a few other odds and ends."

Cheryl's heart fell. "I'm really confused about this whole thing. I don't know. Maybe Naomi and I are on the wrong track."

"Whether you are or not, we still need to find someone who has a reason to frame Mr. Hicks. So far that hasn't happened. And we haven't found anyone who could offer him an alibi that would exonerate him."

"What if all of it is a way to hide the theft of the bear?" Cheryl said slowly. "To muddy the waters?"

The chief stared at her for a moment. "There's an idea. It would explain why the bear is so much different than the rest of the stolen stuff." He frowned at her. "How much is this thing worth?"

Cheryl shrugged. "I'm not exactly sure. Elizabeth is the one who accepted it for our Christmas display. Frankly, in my experience, I'd say it couldn't be more than five hundred dollars."

"People steal things worth that much all the time. Not the crime of the century, but still, five hundred dollars is nothing to sneeze at."

Cheryl thought for a moment. "Yes, but why steal the other items? Why bring Timothy into it?" She shook her head. "I'm just going round and round in circles." She gathered her purse. "I'm sorry to take up your time. I was hoping you would have some information that might lead all of us in the right direction."

"Not yet. But there are just a few days left until I have to send Mr. Hicks to the county jail. If you come up with anything, let me know."

Cheryl was a little surprised by the chief's willingness to listen to her. He might be a little gruff at times, but he was a man of integrity and justice. She knew he didn't want to send Timothy away from Sugarcreek if he wasn't guilty.

As if reading her mind, the chief said, "No matter what I think personally, I owe it to the business owners to follow the evidence. And right now, it's pointin' right at your friend. The missin' stuff was in his possession."

"Chief, can you check the items for fingerprints? See whether or not Timothy ever touched them?"

"I've told you before, Mrs. Miller, this isn't CSI. We don't do that. The county investigators will take care of that."

She stood. "Thanks for making time for me, Chief. I really appreciate it."

"Do you want to speak to Mr. Hicks?"

Although she wanted to, she knew Levi planned to stop by later to check on Timothy. Cheryl wanted to have good news for him, and she didn't yet. "I don't think so. Levi will visit him later today. I'll try to get back in the next couple of days."

The chief nodded. "Okay. Thanks for stoppin' by."

Cheryl hurried out of the station. She'd felt so much better having Naomi's help, but today she wasn't convinced that was going to be enough. It was possible this was one mystery they wouldn't be able to solve.

CHAPTER TWENTY

Cheryl pulled her coat tighter as she exited the police station and made her way to her car. It seemed colder now than when she'd entered the station. Levi had mentioned that a snowstorm was on its way.

She opened her car door and got inside. After starting the engine, she began to wonder if the storm might buy them more time. Maybe it would delay Timothy's transfer to the county jail. She and Naomi couldn't count on that though.

She checked the time. She had to meet Naomi at the Honey Bee in thirty minutes, and before that she needed to pick up the Baby Plays a Lot. She put the car in gear and headed toward the toy store. She'd just turned the corner that led to the store when she saw Mrs. Perry walking down the sidewalk, a cane in one hand and a pet carrier in the other. She stumbled but caught herself before falling. Cheryl quickly pulled over and got out of her car. She jogged up to Mrs. Perry.

"Can I help you?" she asked once she'd reached her.

"Oh, my dear," the elderly woman said, "I'm afraid these old legs of mine aren't quite as strong as they used to be. I would be most grateful for some help."

Cheryl took the pet carrier from her and peeked inside. Grimmy stared back at her and meowed.

"Where are you taking Grimmy?" Cheryl asked.

"I can hardly get the words out," Mrs. Perry said, her voice breaking.

Was she having her precious pet put down? "What do you mean?"

The old woman stopped and grabbed Cheryl's arm. "I'm taking him to Dr. Parker. She's going to do Grimmy's surgery. Some angel stepped up and paid for everything." Tears rolled down her face. "I don't know what I'd do without my Grimmy."

"That…that's wonderful." There it was again. *Some angel.* Of course, the word *angel* was used in a lot of situations. Still, it made her uncomfortable. "Can you tell me about your angel?" she asked Mrs. Perry.

"Dr. Parker said it was anonymous. The person helping my Grimmy doesn't want anyone to know who they are. It's like that scripture. 'Do not let your left hand know what your right hand is doing.'"

"Yes, I understand," Cheryl said. She supported Mrs. Perry's arm, and they started walking again. Dr. Parker's clinic was only two doors away.

"Thank you, honey," Mrs. Perry said as they reached the clinic.

"You're welcome. Let me take Grimmy inside for you."

She opened the door and carried Grimmy into the office. The receptionist greeted them and came around to get the pet carrier.

"He'll be fine, Mrs. Perry," she said. "We'll call you after the surgery."

Mrs. Perry looked upset. "Can't I stay here with him? I don't want him to be afraid."

The receptionist smiled. "Why don't you stay here until after the surgery so the doctor can assure you that everything went well? Grimmy will be sleeping all night after that. You can come back in the morning to pick him up."

"Can someone drive Mrs. Perry home later?" Cheryl asked. "I would hate for her to walk all alone."

"Of course," the receptionist said. "I'll take her myself."

"Is that okay, Mrs. Perry?" Cheryl asked.

"Yes, dear." Mrs. Perry gave her a hug. "Thank you so much. You're an angel too."

Cheryl laughed. "Hardly. I'm going to call you tomorrow and check on Grimmy, okay?"

"That would be nice. And say a prayer for my Grimmy, will you?"

"Absolutely."

Cheryl said goodbye to the receptionist and left. She checked her watch. Only fifteen minutes left until she was supposed to meet Naomi. She hurried to her car, got inside, and drove as quickly as she could to Toys and Treasures, a fairly new store in Sugarcreek. They stocked all the latest toys. The owner, Dodie Price, had moved to Sugarcreek from Des Moines. Besides running the store, she also planned to collect and exhibit antique toys in a museum soon. Cheryl was certain Chief Twitchell had notified Dodie about the stolen bear, but if she had time, she'd ask Dodie if she had any idea why someone would take it and what they could do with it.

She parked and went inside. Thankfully, it wasn't crowded. Only a few harried parents who'd waited until the last moment to get the final gifts for their children—just like her. Actually, she and Levi had picked up almost everything except the doll over a month ago. Amazing, really, since running a farm and taking care of two toddlers kept them so busy.

She looked around for several minutes but didn't see any Baby Plays a Lots. Then she noticed that Dodie had come into the room and had walked behind the counter. Cheryl went over and got her attention.

"Cheryl. Good to see you," Dodie said. "How are you?"

Dodie was a lovely woman with dark hair and dark eyes. Cheryl really liked her. Dodie loved children, and they loved her back. It was great to see someone who truly enjoyed what she did.

"I'm fine," Cheryl said, "but my daughter won't be happy with me if Santa doesn't bring her the number one gift she wants for Christmas."

"Well, that's why we're here. What toy is it she's hoping for?"

"A Baby Plays a Lot. Rebecca noticed them in your window, but I didn't see any on my way inside. Maybe I missed them?"

Dodie's smile slipped. "Oh, Cheryl. I'm so sorry. I've been out of them for over two weeks now. They're one of the most popular toys this year. I tried to get more from the manufacturer, but they're short all over the country."

Although Cheryl had suspected that might be the case, she'd still hoped she could find one. It was her fault. She should have picked it up sooner instead of putting it off. She and Levi had been so unsure about getting Rebecca everything she wanted for Christmas that they'd waited longer than they should have.

"Is there any way to locate one?" she asked. "Maybe in another store in the area? Or someone in town who might be willing to sell theirs?"

"I doubt that, Cheryl, but I'll make a couple of calls. It's not impossible. Sometimes parents buy more than they need, or buy something and then their child asks for something different." She shook her head. "But I wouldn't hold out much hope."

"Maybe I could order one online and pay for expedited shipping."

"Again, I hate to rain on your parade, but my information tells me that no one can get it here before Christmas." She stepped over to a laptop on the counter. "Let me check though." Dodie tapped the keys on her keyboard for a couple of minutes then shook her head. "I don't see anything available anywhere. Again, I'm so, so sorry."

"I should have taken care of it sooner. It's not your fault."

"Is there anything else I could help you find?"

"Yes." She handed Dodie the Christmas request form she'd picked up at the church. Dodie quickly filled it. Thankfully, she had everything the child had requested. "I also need a toy for Matthew. Then I have a question for you."

She smiled. "Let's take the toy first and then the question."

Cheryl told her about the dog dressed like a police officer. Dodie came around the counter and walked over to a display. She picked up a box and brought it back.

"Like this?"

Cheryl breathed a sigh of relief. "Yes, that's it exactly."

"You're lucky. I just got these in. Most places are sold out of these too."

"I'd heard that. I really didn't expect to find it. But then, I didn't expect the doll to be sold out. It seems I don't know my toys."

"Every Christmas is different. I never know what toy is going to be impossible to find and which one I'll end up getting stuck with in inventory. And now for your question?"

"I had an antique stuffed bear stolen from my shop. It's a Gunther, made in the early 1900s."

"Chief Twitchell told me about that. It hasn't turned up yet?"

"No. I'm confused. I understand there aren't that many left in good condition. Wouldn't it be hard for someone to steal and then try to sell without getting caught? How many people would be in the market for it?"

"Unless someone wanted it for their own private collection, it doesn't make any sense. The bear would have to be certified if someone wanted to sell it. And that would make it easy to trace back to the theft here." She frowned. "Depending on its condition, it could be worth anywhere between five hundred to two thousand dollars. More if it's signed, but that's unlikely. I think the more conservative figure is probably right."

"That's still a lot of money if I have to reimburse the Fuszes."

"Maybe the police will find it," Dodie said.

"I hope so."

"Changing the subject, but I heard you and Levi were trying to help that homeless man. I'm sorry it turned out the way it did."

"We don't think he took those things, Dodie. We believe he's being set up."

"Really?" Dodie looked confused. "I don't understand."

"It's a long story, but we're hoping to prove he didn't do it before he's sent to the county jail." Cheryl took out her wallet and removed her credit card to pay for Matthew's police dog and the gifts for the child at church. She handed it to Dodie. "Look, if anyone contacts you about the bear, please let us know immediately. I doubt seriously that anyone is dumb enough to try to sell it in Sugarcreek, but just in case…"

"You have my word, Cheryl. Hey, would you like to see the museum? I'm a lot further along than the last time you were here."

Cheryl glanced at her watch again. "I'd love to, but I'm already ten minutes late meeting Naomi for lunch. I'll stop by after Christmas and check it out. I'm sure it's wonderful."

Dodie handed Cheryl her receipt then bagged the toys. Cheryl thanked her and ran out to her car.

Although she and Naomi were trying to prove Timothy's innocence, the only thing Cheryl could see in her mind at the moment was Rebecca's disappointed expression when she realized Santa had let her down.

CHAPTER TWENTY-ONE

When she got to the Honey Bee, Cheryl hurried inside. The owner, Kathy Kimble, saw her and came to greet her.

"I'm so glad to see you," she said. "It's been a while."

"Too long," Cheryl said with a smile. "I've missed this place—and you."

Kathy was a lovely woman whose welcoming personality helped to make the Honey Bee special.

"Naomi is in the other room," Kathy said. "In a booth."

Cheryl thanked her and headed into the adjoining room. The Honey Bee was a favorite not only with the locals. Visitors from out of town liked to stop by too. Its reputation had been built on its ambience as well as its wonderful and unique menu. But Cheryl's favorite thing about the Honey Bee was Kathy and her friendly, helpful staff. She always felt at home here.

She made her way over to the booth where Naomi waited.

"I'm so sorry," she said breathlessly as she slid into her seat. "I had to stop by the toy store, and on my way there I saw Mrs. Perry walking down the street with Grimmy in his carrier."

"Please don't worry about it," Naomi said. "I knew it was something that could not be helped. You said Mrs. Perry was carrying Grimmy? Where was she going?"

"To the vet. She…"

"The veterinarian?"

Naomi's horrified expression made it clear she had jumped to the same conclusion Cheryl had at first.

"No—I mean yes, but she was taking him to have an operation. One that will make him well."

"Ach, Cheryl. I believe my heart skipped a beat when you said that. I heard Grimmy was ill and that the surgery was expensive. I have been very concerned."

"Someone offered to pay for the entire thing," Cheryl said. "And get this. Mrs. Perry called her benefactor an angel."

"An angel?" Naomi's eyes grew large. "I suppose the term is used in many different circumstances."

"Especially in the last couple of days." Cheryl shook her head. "I'm probably being silly."

"How nice to see you ladies," someone said. Cheryl looked up to see Joanna Stutzman, one of Cheryl's favorite staff members at the Honey Bee. Joanna had naturally silver hair that she kept short. She always had a smile on her face, and her personality shone whenever she walked into a room. Cheryl also liked Joanna's husband, Brian, who was a part-time pastor.

"Nice to see you too," Cheryl said.

"What can I get you to drink?"

Cheryl ordered one of their special lattes. "And I know what I want." She looked at Naomi. "Have you decided?"

"I want the apple, walnut, and cheese sandwich," Naomi said. "And the mushroom soup."

Cheryl laughed. "You're reading my mind." She smiled at Joanna. "I want the exact same thing."

"Good choice," Joanna said. "Perfect for a cold day like today."

Once Joanna walked away, Naomi said, "You went by the toy store? Cutting it a little close, ain't so?"

"Too close," Cheryl said, unable to hide her dismay.

"Is this about that doll Rebecca wants so badly?"

Cheryl nodded. "They're sold out. Have been for weeks. Rebecca is going to be so disappointed. Levi and I have been trying to teach her the real meaning of Christmas, but it's been hard to make her understand it when all the other children she's around talk constantly about what they're getting. Although yesterday when she was playing with some of the other children at church, she offered to give her doll to another little girl who might not get one. I guess now they'll both have to be disappointed."

"I am sorry, Cheryl. If I could get the doll for Rebecca, I would."

Cheryl had to smile at Naomi's comment. She knew her mother-in-law meant it, although many in the Amish community would consider the doll not only inappropriate but also an unnecessary luxury.

Joanna brought Cheryl's caramel latte. She sighed as she picked it up and took a sip. The latte warmed her and actually made her feel a little better.

"Maybe Rebecca's angel will bring her the doll," she said. "At least I can hope."

She started to say something else when someone who'd exited the booth behind Naomi stopped at their table—Pastor Brotton and the newcomer Judith.

"It's nice to see you both," Pastor Brotton said.

"You too, Pastor," Cheryl said. "And Judith, how are you?"

The woman was dressed in vintage clothing, just like yesterday. Cheryl introduced her to Naomi.

"I'm so happy to meet you," Judith said. "Pastor Brotton was nice enough to treat me to lunch. He's regaled me with the most interesting stories about the history of the church. Some of his tales are downright funny."

"I'm sure they are," Cheryl said with a smile. "We may have been involved in some of them."

"I don't think he mentioned you. He's very protective of the people who attend Community Bible Church. You're blessed to have such an amazing pastor."

"I think so too," Cheryl said.

"We'd better get going before my head gets too big for my shoulders," Pastor Brotton said.

Judith laughed. "It was nice to see you again, Cheryl, and very nice to meet you, Naomi."

"Thank you," Naomi said. "I hope we will see each other again."

"That would be nice. Goodbye."

Joanna came up to the table with their lunches, a smile on her face. "Kathy says this is on the house."

"She doesn't need to do that," Cheryl said.

Joanna laughed. "You can tell her that, but when she makes up her mind…"

Cheryl grinned. "Okay. I get it. Tell her thank you."

"You bet."

As Joanna walked away, Naomi shook her head. "This is getting silly. We go to lunch, yet no one allows us to pay. I never thought we were that special. I feel like some kind of celebrity."

Cheryl laughed. "If we're the only celebrities Sugarcreek has… Well, that's just sad."

Naomi smiled. "I believe you are right about that. Kathy is such a nice person."

"Yes, she is. I've missed it here."

"Ja, as have I."

They ate silently for a few minutes. The sandwich was an explosion of flavors that melded together to create something unique and delicious. And the mushroom soup certainly was different than the kind from a can.

"So what did Chief Twitchell have to say?" Naomi asked after swallowing a spoonful of soup.

"Nothing helpful. I think he's really hoping we'll turn up something that will make it easier on him."

"I would like to fulfill his hopes," Naomi said with a sigh.

"Me too. Did you stop by Kasey's store?"

Naomi nodded. "Oh my. That woman." She sighed again. "I try to show love to everyone, but it took all the Christian love I could muster to be kind to her."

"What do you mean?"

"She was interested in carrying my food items in her store, but only if I discounted them so low I would only make pennies on the dollar."

"Why am I not surprised?"

"Because you are wise about people," Naomi said.

"Did you find out anything helpful?"

"No, not really. But I can tell you that her employees do not respect her, and as Esther told you, the items in her store are cheap imitations of real Amish crafts and foods. I was not impressed. I managed to mention some of the thefts in Sugarcreek. That certainly evoked a reaction. She has had a few things go missing, she says. I also brought up Timothy, and she acted as if she is convinced he is the one who has taken items from her store. But when I specifically asked if she had seen him in her store, she got flustered and changed the subject."

"That's odd."

"She is a very odd woman. And her clerk, Dallas? He kept his eye on me the entire time I was there. As if he thought I might suddenly pull out a gun and hold up their store."

Cheryl laughed. "I don't think I've ever heard you talk like that about someone."

"I am sorry, but that woman definitely got my goat." Naomi took a bite of her sandwich. Once she'd swallowed, she said, "I think we should continue to research her. She could be involved somehow with framing your friend."

"I have an idea," Cheryl said. "I'll find a way to get some pictures of Kasey and Dallas. Then Levi can take them to the jail and show them to Timothy. See if he recognizes them."

"That is a wonderful idea, Cheryl. If he does, it would help us immensely."

"And if he doesn't?" Cheryl asked.

"Well, we have not lost anything, ain't so?"

"I suppose not." Cheryl wiped her mouth with her napkin. "Oh, by the way, have you talked to the Fuszes about the bear? I still want to speak to them myself. To apologize."

"Ja, I went by to see them this morning on my way to town. Even though the bear had sentimental value, they do not blame you. They told me that the bear was insured." She frowned.

"Is something wrong?"

"I do not know. It is just…"

"What?"

"Mrs. Fusz asked her husband how much he had insured the bear for. At first he declined to answer. But finally he told her it was insured for…" Naomi looked a little confused before she said, "Five thousand dollars."

CHAPTER TWENTY-TWO

Cheryl stared at Naomi in surprise. Five thousand dollars? Didn't Dodie say the old cloth bear might be worth only between five hundred and two thousand dollars?

"I don't understand," she said. "If I'd known it was worth that much, I never would have accepted it."

Naomi leaned closer as if she feared someone was listening. "And if I had known, I would have advised you not to accept it."

Cheryl frowned at her. "Were you afraid to tell me about this?"

"Do you mean why did I wait until now to bring it up?"

Cheryl nodded.

"I wish I could answer your question. I have been turning the information over and over in my mind, not sure what to think. I do not want to accuse people I consider friends…"

The look on Naomi's face made it clear that she was having the same thoughts Cheryl was.

"You think the Fuszes might have staged the thefts so they could get the insurance money? That they may have set this whole thing up?"

"I do not like wondering if this could be true. You know them. How can I believe this?"

"Maybe they took the bear so they could get the insurance money, but that doesn't necessarily mean this is connected to Timothy."

"That may be true, but the timing is very convenient, ain't so?" Naomi shook her head. "I have gone back and forth about this. I do not know my own mind. That is why I hesitated to tell you what I heard." She shrugged. "Perhaps the bear really is worth that much. Maybe it really was stolen. It is possible."

"Yes, it's possible. But—"

"I know, I know. The timing is suspicious."

"I think we need to tell Chief Twitchell about this. Let him look into it."

"Another reason I did not want to say anything," Naomi said, her voice shaking. "How can I turn in my friends?"

The Fuszes were longtime Sugarcreek residents. At one time they'd owned a small grocery store that specialized in Amish foods. Even though they weren't Amish, the community respected them, and many Amish people sold their goods in their store.

"It's the chief's job to sort everything out," Cheryl said. "Herschel and Nettie will be given fair treatment. You know that." She paused. "Wait a minute, did you say that Nettie asked Herschel how much *he* insured the bear for?"

"Ja, that is right."

"Maybe she's not involved."

"And maybe neither one is guilty."

Naomi's tone was sharp, not like her at all. Cheryl realized how upset she was. What should they do? Was this connected to Timothy or not? There was no way to know.

"Before we do anything else, let's research the bear. Maybe Dodie was wrong. If she was, it means we're suspicious of the Fuszes for nothing. But if we find out the bear isn't worth five thousand dollars, we have to tell Chief Twitchell."

"The chief has not always been impartial, you know." Naomi sighed and leaned back in her seat.

"Don't worry, Naomi. At least not until we know the truth."

"All right." Naomi straightened up and reached for her cup. "I wish I could go back in time and refuse their offer of the bear for your Christmas display."

Cheryl couldn't help but chuckle. "Unless you have a time machine stashed somewhere, that's not going to happen."

She didn't know what to tell her friend. Naomi was usually more upbeat and positive. The situation with the Fuszes was really bothering her. Or was it something else?

"You're still thinking of Sarah, aren't you?"

A tear slipped down Naomi's face, and she quickly wiped it away. "Ja. I am sorry. I cannot figure out why I feel her absence so deeply this year." The corners of her mouth twitched up. "Esther says it is because the answer to my prayers is right around the corner and the devil is angry." She smiled at Cheryl. "I do not know where she gets these things. I suspect much of it comes from Lydia."

"How about some cinnamon crumb cake," a voice said, making Cheryl jump. She looked up to see Joanna standing next to their booth. Cheryl had been so focused on Naomi she hadn't noticed Joanna approach.

"I'm not sure." She looked at Naomi and smiled. "Do you feel like having a piece?"

Naomi nodded. "I think it is exactly what I need to chase away the blues."

"I agree. Two pieces and two more coffees, please, Joanna. But only if Kathy will allow us to pay for it."

Joanna laughed. "I'll write you a separate ticket for the coffee cake. She'll never know. It will be our secret."

"Okay, thanks."

"I'm sorry you're having the blues," Joanna said to Naomi. "I'll pray for you."

"Thank you so much," Naomi said to her. "You are a blessing."

"I appreciate that, but praying for each other should be second nature for us." She granted them another of her brilliant smiles and headed for the kitchen.

As soon as she left, Cheryl pulled out her phone and did a brief search of stuffed bears made by the German company. Although she didn't sell antique toys in the Swiss Miss, she had seen several of the bears down through the years. Most of them weren't very valuable. Was this one the exception? A brief search didn't reveal the bear taken from her shop.

"Did you find anything?" Naomi asked as Cheryl put her phone back into her purse.

"No, not really. Some of the bears have increased in value, but most are worth about the same amount we assumed the Fuszes' bear is worth. I'll do more research when I get home."

Naomi took a bite of her cake. "There may be one other suspect to add to our list," she said slowly.

Cheryl washed a bite of her coffee cake down with her coffee. "And who would that be?"

"What about Dodie? We know she is trying to start a museum with old toys. What if she wanted the bear for her museum?"

"But she wouldn't be able to display it," Cheryl said. "Everyone would know she took it."

"Maybe not. What if she claimed it was a different bear? Is there anything distinctive about the stolen bear? Something that would identify it?"

"As a matter of fact, there is. A tag with a number on it."

"So there's no way she could get away with the theft."

Naomi's comment wasn't a question. It was a statement of fact. But now Cheryl's mind was spinning. Were they reaching? Dodie didn't seem like the kind of person to take things that didn't belong to her. Cheryl just couldn't accept that. Yet it was strange that the bear went missing at the same time Dodie opened an antique toy museum. Was it really coincidence?

"I am sorry, Cheryl," Naomi said suddenly. "I have put suspicion in your mind toward Dodie, a woman you trust. I should not have done that."

"Don't be silly. You only brought up a good point. And you're right. She is someone we need to look at. I hadn't considered her until you said something." She frowned and ran her finger around the rim of her coffee cup. "What if I find out that the bear is worth five thousand dollars? That would mean Dodie lied to me. I mean, if anyone should know its value, she should, right?"

"I suppose so," Naomi said. "I admit to being somewhat confused. The only thing I cannot get out of my mind is that the thefts at the other shops and the missing bear might not be connected at all. Perhaps this is why the bear was not found in the dawdy haus."

Which in Cheryl's mind could point to Herschel and Nettie Fusz being involved in the theft of the bear. But she wasn't going to bring that up again. At least not until she found out the value of the bear.

As they finished their lunch, Cheryl couldn't help but feel unsettled. Naomi was uncomfortable thinking her friends, the Fuszes, were guilty of insurance fraud. And now Cheryl was having doubts about Dodie, a woman she considered a friend.

When they found out the truth, would the impact be a lot more personal than they'd ever imagined?

Chapter Twenty-Three

After lunch Cheryl swung by the grocery store. She picked up what she needed and was in the checkout line when she heard someone behind her call her name. She turned around and came face-to-face with Herschel and Nettie Fusz.

"Hello, dear," Nettie said.

Although Cheryl had known the elderly couple for years, she hadn't had much interaction with Herschel. She knew Nettie from women's gatherings she'd gone to with Naomi, and, of course, Nettie was a frequent visitor to the Swiss Miss.

Cheryl left her cart and walked back to where the couple stood. "I'm so sorry about the bear. I wanted to come to you right away, but Naomi felt that she should be the person who told you since you'd given it to her in the first place."

"Oh, honey," Nettie said, "Naomi explained what happened. You can't be held responsible for someone who decides to take something that doesn't belong to them." She sighed. "We didn't think it through very well. It's just that the bear has been sitting on a shelf for so many years, and when I saw the lovely display you were working on, I thought it would look perfect under your tree. I was convinced your customers would enjoy seeing our Bertie Bear."

Bertie Bear? They'd named it? "And they did," Cheryl said. "We had several comments on it. The children really loved it." The person in line in front of her moved up a space, so Cheryl took a couple of steps and pushed her cart forward. Then she went back to her conversation with the Fuszes.

"I'm so glad the children enjoyed him," Nettie said. "Just like I did when I was little."

"It was yours when you were young?" Cheryl asked. She'd gotten it into her head that the bear was simply some kind of investment. But now it seemed that Nettie had an emotional attachment to it. Cheryl's feelings of guilt were growing with every second.

"Yes, dear," Nettie said. "But I'm old. When I die I can't take him with me. Things are just things, after all. I just wanted others to appreciate him."

"Naomi said it was insured."

"Yeah, we'll get the money back," Herschel said, his tone sharp. "But Dolly has lost something important to her, no matter how she makes it sound."

"Herschel!" Nettie said. "I do not want you to make this poor girl feel guilty. The person who should feel guilty is the one who took it."

Herschel muttered something under his breath. Cheryl couldn't make it all out, but she understood the word *irresponsible.* Now she felt really terrible.

"Hey, lady, do you mind?" Cheryl looked behind the Fuszes and saw a woman with a cart glaring at her.

Cheryl turned around to see that the line had cleared and the cashier was waiting for her, a deep frown on her face.

"I want you to know that the police are aware of the theft," she said hurriedly. "They're looking for the bear. And so am I."

Cheryl pushed her cart up to the cashier, quickly unloaded her groceries, and paid for them. Then she said goodbye to the Fuszes and hurried to her car. After putting the groceries in the back of her car, she slid inside and pulled out of the parking lot, not wanting to run into the elderly couple again. Her suspicions about Herschel and his "Dolly" being responsible for the theft of the bear had certainly lessened. Herschel seemed sincerely upset about the missing toy, and even though Nettie was being kind and understanding, it was clear that losing the bear bothered her.

Before she headed home, she swung by the Swiss Miss. She jogged up to the door and went inside. Elizabeth was checking someone out, so Cheryl waited until she was finished. She waved at Lydia, who was helping a woman looking at homemade Christmas decorations.

When Elizabeth's customer walked away, Cheryl stepped up to the counter. "Did you see the Fuszes in here after we put their bear in our display?"

Elizabeth frowned as she considered Cheryl's question. "Ja," she said slowly after a few seconds. "They were here because they wanted to see it. They were very happy about how the bear was bringing joy to people. Especially children."

"And how long was this before the bear went missing?"

Again, Elizabeth was quiet as she considered Cheryl's question. Finally, she shook her head. "I do not know. I think maybe a couple of days after the display went up? But I cannot be sure. They did not buy anything. If they had, I could look up the date."

"That's okay. I was just curious."

Elizabeth leaned forward and lowered her voice. "You do not suspect them of stealing their own bear, do you? What good would that do?"

"No, I'm not saying they took it," Cheryl said, looking around to see if anyone could hear them. Thankfully, Lydia and her customer were still talking about the decorations. "I'm just trying to figure out who was in the shop before the bear was taken. Kasey and her employee were both in here before the bear disappeared, right?"

"You and Maam are trying to figure out who took the bear, ain't so?" She grinned. "So the chase is afoot?"

Cheryl chuckled.

"I thought the homeless man, Timothy, was responsible," Elizabeth said. "Maam said he has been arrested."

"Yes, he has, but I don't think he did it." She sighed. "If only one of us had noticed when it disappeared." She put her hand on Elizabeth's arm. "I'm not blaming you at all. I was in here several times after the bear was added to the display, and I can't tell you when it was taken either. At least you have an excuse. You were busy with customers. I can't claim that." She removed her hand and straightened up. "I've got to get home. Levi will be waiting on me."

She said goodbye, went out to her car, and headed home so Levi could get to the jail and visit Timothy. She could hardly wait to get out her laptop and research the missing bear. The question was, what if it wasn't worth five thousand dollars? What if her discovery made Herschel and Nettie look guilty? The couple was loved by many of the residents in Sugarcreek. If she told the police her suspicions, and they were innocent, would the town turn against her?

Chapter Twenty-Four

Once Cheryl arrived at home, after unloading her groceries and putting them away, she put Matthew down for a nap and Rebecca in front of the TV to watch her favorite children's show. Levi wasn't too keen about having the TV on too much, but during the day the children were allowed one show. Matthew loved the cartoon with the police officer puppy, and Rebecca was in love with a show featuring a pig who spoke with an English accent. Levi had pointed out the absurdity of both scenarios until Cheryl told him that when she was little she'd watched a show with a giant yellow bird, a vampire that taught children how to count, and a grouchy green character who lived in a trash can. She still laughed when she recalled the look on his face. After that he never complained about the children's choices.

Once she was sure Matthew was drifting off, she set her laptop on the kitchen table. After searching online for a while, she still didn't have an answer. None of the bears looked exactly like the one owned by the Fuszes. She finally wrote down the phone number of a dealer who seemed to specialize in collectible stuffed animals. She wished she'd made a note of the information on the bear's tag when Nettie dropped it off at the shop, but she hadn't thought it was important then.

She uploaded the photo she'd taken of the display from her phone to her laptop then took a couple of minutes to check an online site that shared items for sale in Sugarcreek. It was a long shot, but she couldn't get the doll Rebecca wanted off her mind. Her little girl was convinced that Santa was going to bring her a Baby Plays a Lot. Even though she and Levi kept emphasizing the importance of using Christmas as a way to celebrate the birth of Jesus, they both understood the excitement of a child at Christmas. Levi's family exchanged gifts too, but they were simple. Still, Levi remembered being excited about receiving Christmas presents. His father carved wonderful toys for the boys while their mother made dolls and doll clothes for the girls. These were the same toys that Rebecca and Matthew still played with. Each child also received a new article of clothing and a pair of shoes. The meals and the desserts added to their holiday joy. The Amish also celebrated Old Christmas on January sixth. They played games and ate delicious food.

Cheryl was scrolling through the site when suddenly the doll popped up on the screen. She was so surprised to see it that she froze for a moment. The site was taking bids on the doll, but the bidding was going to stop in less than two minutes. There was no way to tell what anyone else was bidding. Cheryl put in a bid she felt she and Levi could live with. Thirty seconds before the bidding was set to end, she raised her bid. She wasn't sure how Levi would feel about it, but her heart was focused on her little girl. It was her fault for waiting to buy the doll, and she wanted to fix her mistake if she could.

Cheryl watched as the seconds ticked down. 10…9…8…7…6…5…4…3…2…1. She held her breath, waiting to see who won. Then a message popped up on her screen. *Sorry, your bid was not accepted.*

Cheryl's heart dropped. She spent a few more minutes searching the site for another doll, but it was fruitless. Rebecca's laughter drifted into the kitchen, and it made Cheryl feel even worse. It was Wednesday. Only four more days until Christmas. Even if she could find another doll online, it would never get here in time. She had to give up. On Christmas morning she'd be explaining to Rebecca why Santa had let her down. It wasn't a conversation she was looking forward to.

She got up and started the coffee maker. Even though the house was warm, in the winter she almost always felt cold. After getting her coffee and adding pumpkin-spiced coffee creamer, she went back to the table and picked up her phone to call the expert she'd found online.

The phone rang four times before someone picked up. The woman who answered was the very expert she wanted to talk to. She was surprised. She assumed she'd get a clerk or an assistant. After explaining the situation, the woman seemed eager to help.

"Believe it or not, this isn't the first time that owners of valuable toys have reported them stolen so they could get the insurance money. Of course, this makes them impossible to sell for several years. Most toy collectors keep close tabs on supposedly stolen items so they can notify the authorities if someone offers it for sale."

"I'm so grateful for your help," Cheryl said. "I know people must ask you for appraisals all the time."

"Yes, they do, but your situation is different. I really want to help you. Tell me what you can about the bear."

"I can not only tell you, I can show you. I took a picture of the display. But what I can't do is show you the tag. From what I've found online, the bears are numbered and the number is on the tag."

"That's true, but even without that number I think I can give you a pretty good estimate. Why don't you send me the picture first? That might save you from trying to describe it to me."

"It's not a great photo, but I can do that."

The woman gave Cheryl her email address, and Cheryl sent the photo to her. It only took a few moments to complete the task.

"I've got it," she said. She was quiet for a moment before saying, "This is a Gunther bear. Medium size. It was made in the nineteen thirties in Germany. It looks as if it's in excellent condition. Is that what you observed?"

"Yes. The woman who owns it said it's been sitting on a shelf for many years."

"All right. Now, as you said, if I knew the number on the tag, I could give you a more exact appraisal, so don't hold me to this."

"I understand. Just a realistic range is all I really need. If it's close to the insurance amount, I won't pursue this any further."

"Now let me say one thing before I give you my guess at its worth. Sometimes an amount is added to an insurance policy because the item can't be replaced. Depending on the number on the tag, that could figure in here somewhere."

"Okay." Cheryl realized she was holding her breath.

"I would say the bear is worth around twenty-five hundred dollars. And that's only possible if it's in excellent condition. Since I can only see part of it, I'm guessing at that. Now, if the number on its tag shows it's one of Gunther's early bears, you could add another thousand to that."

"That's still quite a bit less than the five thousand it's insured for."

"Yes, but again, this is the best I can do without actually seeing the bear and looking it over. However, I believe what I told you is pretty accurate."

"Thank you so much. I truly appreciate your help."

"You're welcome. Send me an email sometime and let me know how it turned out, okay?"

"I will. Merry Christmas."

"Merry Christmas to you too."

Cheryl put the phone down and sat there for a moment before picking up the phone again to call the police department.

CHAPTER TWENTY-FIVE

After picking her phone up and putting it down several times, Cheryl finally punched in the numbers and listened to the phone ring. A few seconds later Delores answered. "Sugarcreek Police Department, can I help you?"

Cheryl took a deep breath. "Delores, it's Cheryl Miller. Is the chief around?"

"As a matter of fact, he is. I'll put you through."

Great. The one time she hoped he wouldn't be there, he was. She tried to build up her courage as his phone rang. She liked the Fuszes. Suggesting they were involved in fraud was difficult for her. She thought about ending the call a couple of times, but before she could act on the impulse, the chief answered.

"Chief Twitchell," he said.

"It's Cheryl Miller."

"Yeah, I know. Delores told me. What can I do for you, Cheryl?"

"Look, Chief, I'm not sure this means anything, but I feel I need to tell you about Herschel and Nettie Fusz. They insured that stuffed bear for five thousand dollars. But I talked to an expert today who said it was only worth half that amount. I'm not sure, but I'm concerned that they might have committed insurance fraud."

"You mean you think they took their own bear so they could collect the insurance money?"

"I think it's possible. To be honest, I have a hard time believing that. But I had to tell you about it."

"So you think the thefts from our local shops and the missing bear are two different crimes?"

"Maybe," Cheryl said. "I mean, why wasn't it with the rest of the stolen items?"

"It's possible, I guess." The chief sighed. "Okay, I'll check on it, maybe call Herschel and Nettie in and talk to them."

"Please, Chief, don't tell them I told you about this, okay?"

Chief Twitchell was quiet for a moment. Then he said, "I'll try, but I can't control who they'd suspect on their own."

"I understand."

When Cheryl ended the call, she felt sick to her stomach. What had she done? She tried to remind herself that she hadn't done anything wrong. But if that was true, why did she feel like this?

She looked at the clock on her kitchen wall. Rebecca's show would be ending soon. Cheryl picked up her phone again and called Naomi. Their bishop had approved cell phones for those who had a business, as well as for farmers who spent a lot of time in the fields. They'd decided that in cases of emergency their families needed to be able to contact them.

"Hello," Naomi said, picking up on the first ring.

Cheryl told her about her call to Chief Twitchell.

"Oh my," she said. "All right. Thank you for letting me know. I am afraid that if the chief calls them into the station to talk to them, Herschel and Nettie will think I am the one who contacted him."

"And I'm afraid they'll know it was me," Cheryl said with a sigh. "Did I do the wrong thing? Would you have called the police if you were me?"

"That is hard to say," Naomi said slowly. "If the Fuszes were Amish, I most definitely would not have. We deal with this kind of situation internally, and I would report it to the bishop and the elders." She sighed. "But the Fuszes are not Amish, and you did the only thing you could do. You have an obligation to Chief Twitchell to tell him what you know."

The confidence in Naomi's response left Cheryl feeling a little better. "All right. I just wanted you to know about this in case Herschel or Nettie say something."

"I appreciate that. If anything else happens, please let me know."

"I will."

After Cheryl ended the call, she took a deep breath and let it out slowly, trying to calm herself. Naomi was right. She had told the chief she would report back to him any information she discovered in her research of the case. After that, it was up to him what he did with it. She glanced at the clock again. She planned on making meat loaf for supper. She got up from her chair and took onions and green peppers out of the fridge. She was chopping them when Rebecca came into the room.

"Mama, can I feed Bun Bun now?"

"Let's wait until I get these vegetables chopped, okay? It will only take me a few minutes."

"Why can't I feed Bun Bun by myself? Is it because of the angel?"

"Have you seen this angel again?"

Rebecca shook her head, a solemn expression on her face. "I think angels only come when you want them. You and Daddy don't like the angel."

Cheryl stopped chopping, wiped her hands, and sat down at the kitchen table. "Come here, Boo," she said gently.

Rebecca came over to her, and Cheryl took her hands. "Daddy and I like angels, but we think the person you saw the other night was a real person. She might even have something to do with something bad that happened to Timothy, our friend."

Rebecca frowned. "Timothy isn't my friend. I don't really know him."

Cheryl was surprised by her daughter's declaration. She'd never heard her say anything like that before. Then she remembered saying the same thing when talking to Esther about Timothy. They'd been in the Swiss Miss, and Rebecca had been with her. She must have overheard her. What should she say now? She didn't want Rebecca to be suspicious of everyone she didn't know. But at the same time, she wanted her little girl to be careful when it came to strangers.

"Daddy and Mama know him, Boo. You're right not to trust everyone, but sometimes we have to take a risk and trust some people."

"Should I trust Timothy then?"

Cheryl stared into her innocent daughter's eyes. "I believe so, yes."

"But I shouldn't trust the angel?"

Oh, brother. "Look, let's talk about this later with Daddy, okay? I think he might have a wonderful answer to your question."

"Okay," Rebecca said slowly. "Daddy is pretty smart, isn't he?"

Cheryl smiled at her. "Yes, he is."

Rebecca frowned. "Aren't you smart, Mama?"

Oh, great. "Yes, Rebecca. I think I'm smart, but sometimes problems come out better when Daddy and I work on things together. There's a famous expression that goes 'two heads are better than one.'"

Rebecca's eyes grew wide. "Oh, Mama. I don't want you to have two heads. You would be a monster!"

Cheryl bit her lip to keep from laughing. "No, honey. That doesn't mean that one person has two heads. It means that two people thinking about something together have a better chance of coming up with the right answer."

Rebecca still looked a little confused. Frankly, Cheryl was beginning to feel the same way. "You can go out to the barn and feed Bun Bun. I'll be there in a minute. I know you can feed him by yourself, but I want to see him too. Is that okay?"

"Sure, Mama. I guess so." Rebecca trounced out of the kitchen, heading toward the door.

"Don't forget your coat!" Cheryl called after her.

She heard a loud sigh from her obviously upset daughter. *Is this a preview of what it will be like when she's a teenager?* Cheryl wondered. She heard the front door open and close. She finished chopping her vegetables, and then she put them aside and went to check on Matthew. He was still asleep. She couldn't leave him alone for long, but she wouldn't be gone more than a couple of minutes. She didn't want Rebecca outside alone.

She got her coat and stepped through the doorway. The cold hit her in the face and almost took her breath away. The promised snowstorm was getting closer, and the sky was full of dark clouds that seemed to be a portent of things to come.

A blast of wind pushed her along as she made her way to the barn. She opened the door and found Rebecca putting food into Bun Bun's hutch. His leg seemed to be improving. Cheryl was really relieved, but when the day came to release him, she wasn't sure Rebecca would understand. She really loved him.

The barn was warm and comfortable. Cheryl checked on the horses. Sampson put his large head on her shoulder as she stroked his face. They loved their horses and were grateful that Seth and Naomi had given the Morgans to them. Seth had made a big deal about how he needed younger horses, but she and Levi knew giving the horses away was a big sacrifice for them.

"I'm done," Rebecca said as she closed and locked Bun Bun's hutch.

Cheryl stroked Sampson's face one more time and started to follow her daughter out of the barn when she saw something that caused her to stop in her tracks.

Sitting on a bale of hay near the barn door was the Fuszes' stuffed bear.

Chapter Twenty-Six

Cheryl froze in place for a moment, trying to understand what she was seeing. How in the world did the bear get there? It wasn't in the barn yesterday. And it couldn't have been there last night when Levi fed the horses. He would have noticed it. Someone either broke into their barn late last night while they were sleeping or sometime today. Was it while she was gone or after she got home? No matter when it happened, it was frightening. Someone had been on their property. Was that person here now?

Cheryl grabbed Rebecca's arm with one hand and the bear with the other. Then she pulled Rebecca out of the barn and dragged her toward the house. Were they being watched? She was aware Rebecca was frightened, but so was she.

"I'm sorry," she told her tearful child. "We've got to get inside right now."

They ran to the house. Once they were inside, Cheryl locked the front door. Then she hurried to the back door and locked that as well.

"Mama, is the monster with two heads gonna get us?"

"Oh, Rebecca," Cheryl said breathlessly, "I told you there are no monsters with two heads. Look, everything's all right. I just need to call someone." At that moment, Matthew cried out from his room. Super, just what she needed.

She was headed for his room when she realized she still had her coat on. She took it off and put it over one of the chairs at the kitchen table. Then she helped Rebecca out of hers and placed it on top of her own.

"Mama, the coats don't go there," Rebecca declared. "You're doing it wrong."

Cheryl took a deep breath. "I'll take care of them in a minute," she told Rebecca, trying to keep her voice steady. "Why don't you go watch TV while Mama takes care of a couple of things, okay?"

Once again Rebecca's eyes grew wide. "Daddy said not too much TV."

Cheryl had finally had enough. "Rebecca, go to your room. Now. I mean it."

The little girl's bottom lip trembled, and she fled to her bedroom, closing the door behind her. Cheryl felt guilty for being so short with her, but she needed a few minutes to think.

She went into Matthew's room and helped him out of bed. Then she grabbed her phone and called the police station. Thankfully, Levi was still there.

"Stay in the house with the doors locked," he told her. "And hold on while I tell someone what happened."

"Okay."

Matthew began to pull on Cheryl's pant leg, asking for a snack. She put the phone on speaker, hurried into the kitchen, and grabbed a banana. She cut it up and led her son into the living room, where she turned on the TV.

"Sit here and eat your banana," she said.

"Puppy...puppy...puppy...," Matthew began to say over and over.

"Matty, it isn't time for the puppy show. Watch this one until the puppy show comes on, okay?"

Tears filled his eyes. "Puppy...puppy...puppy."

"Cheryl?" Levi's voice came through her phone. "Are you there?"

"Yes." She fought back tears. She was frightened, and both her children were crying. This was ridiculous.

"I am on my way home, and an officer will follow me."

"All right. Rebecca and Matthew are both upset, and I need to take care of them."

"All right. But do not hang up. It will take us a while to get there, and I want to make certain you are safe."

"I appreciate that, Levi. I really do."

"Did the children see something that upset them?" Levi asked.

Cheryl sighed. "No. It seems that suggesting Rebecca watch TV for a few minutes is horrifying because 'Daddy said not too much TV.' And if the show doesn't have Matthew's puppy, it's the supreme betrayal."

Even though Cheryl knew Levi was concerned about his family, she heard him chuckle. Somehow it made her feel better. She took a deep breath. The truth was, she felt fairly certain that whoever had left the bear was gone. She couldn't fathom why the thief would return the bear, but she was grateful it was back. It certainly proved that Timothy hadn't taken it. He was in jail. There was no way he could have done it.

Although her mind wanted to pick apart this new turn of events, right now Rebecca and Matthew came first. She went into the living room and picked up the TV remote. She'd saved a movie they'd watched a couple of months ago that starred Matthew's puppy. She clicked on the movie, and Matthew's tears turned into smiles.

Then she went to Rebecca's bedroom. She opened the door and found her daughter curled up on her bed, still crying. Cheryl sat down next to her and stroked her hair.

"I'm sorry, Boo," she said gently. "There was something important that Mama needed to do. That's why I asked you to watch TV for a few minutes so I could take care of it. I didn't mean to upset you."

"Are you mad at me?"

"Of course not, honey. I was worried about something else."

"About the bear?"

Cheryl nodded. "Yes, it had to do with the bear."

"And about the monster with two heads?"

If only she could take back those words. "No, Boo. Like I told you, there are no monsters with two heads."

"But you said—"

"Forget what I said. Sometimes mamas and daddies say the wrong things."

"But, Mama, Daddy said what he says goes."

Cheryl, who at this point knew there was no winning this argument, went to the only defense she had. The words "Would you like a cookie?" slipped out of her mouth before she could stop them.

Cheryl was grateful to see her daughter break out into a smile. "Yes, please. Thank you, Mama."

Impressed that Rebecca had worked both *please* and *thank you* into her response, Cheryl felt the relief that victory finally brought.

Even though the TV was on, somehow Matthew's two-year-old ears were able to hear the word *cookie*.

"Me too?" he asked as he walked into Rebecca's room. "I want cookie."

Cheryl, whose stomach had been tied up in knots, laughed. "Yes, maybe even two cookies."

Rebecca frowned. "Mama, Daddy says—"

"Yes, I know. But I can promise you that Daddy wouldn't mind me giving you two cookies right now."

Although Rebecca looked a little confused, the promise of a couple of cookies trumped her father's house rules about too many sweets.

"Come on, you two sillies. Let's get cookies. I need one too."

Her giggling children hurried out of the bedroom and made a beeline toward the kitchen. Cheryl stopped for a moment and stared at the bear she'd put on the bookshelf. Its reappearance was a mystery but one that would keep for a few minutes. Right now, all she wanted was to give her children cookies and milk.

Chapter Twenty-Seven

It didn't take long for Levi and Chief Twitchell to get there. Cheryl was surprised that the chief had come instead of sending one of his officers.

Levi sent Rebecca and Matthew to Rebecca's bedroom to play while they spoke to the chief.

"I don't think there's much I can do," the chief said, looking over the bear. "It wouldn't do any good to send it on to the county and have them look it over for fingerprints. This fur would keep fingerprints from showing up. Although DNA is possible, it's not likely the person who took the bear left anything the lab could use. Even if that had happened, the perp's DNA would have to be in the database. That's a long shot." He frowned at Cheryl. "You didn't hear anything? Didn't see anybody?"

"No, I didn't notice a thing. Didn't hear anyone."

The chief stood up from the table. "I'm goin' out there to look around. Why don't you come with me, Levi? I could use some help."

It was already getting dark outside. The chief had his own flashlight, and he encouraged Levi to get one too. Together they went outside and headed toward the barn.

After they left, Cheryl went into the kitchen to put the meat loaf together and get it into the oven. They'd be eating a little later than usual tonight, but there wasn't much she could do about it. She was startled when Beau began to meow. At first she didn't see him, but then she realized he was sitting by his food bowls.

"I'm sorry. I forgot to feed you," she said, shaking her head. "Just a minute, Beau. Let me get this in the oven."

As if he understood her, he stopped meowing and sat quietly, waiting patiently for his food. She smiled at him. "You're such a good guy, you know that?" He dipped his head, as if acknowledging her praise, which made her laugh.

A few minutes later she had the meat loaf in the oven, so she picked up Beau's dish and checked his water. Then she got a can of his favorite food out of the pantry. He loved anything tuna flavored. She opened the can and dumped it into his bowl while he rubbed up against her legs, purring.

She'd just put his bowl on the floor when the front door opened. Levi and the chief came into the kitchen, and Chief Twitchell removed his hat. "Something smells…interesting," he said.

Cheryl laughed. "Cat food."

Levi feigned a sigh of relief and wiped his forehead.

The chief smiled. "I'm glad. I was feelin' real sorry for your family."

"You two are hilarious. Did you find anything?"

Levi, who was hanging up his coat, shook his head. "We looked for tracks from a person or a vehicle, but the ground is too hard. We could not find anything helpful."

Cheryl leaned against the counter. "So now what?" she asked the chief.

"Well, I think you can return the bear to the Fuszes."

"This doesn't mean they weren't planning to defraud their insurance company," Cheryl said.

"So they brought it over here and left it with you?" the chief asked incredulously. "Tell me how that makes any sense."

"Well…" Cheryl tried to find a scenario that would work. She could only come up with one possibility. "Okay, so they took the bear, hid it, and were going to report it to their insurance company, but then they had an attack of conscience and brought it here."

"Why here?" the chief asked.

"Um… Well, they couldn't take it back to my shop or say they just found it. They needed a neutral place to drop it off."

"And your barn's a neutral place?" He shook his head. "I don't think so. Puttin' it here only brings up questions. Why not say someone dropped it out at their place? Makin' it look like what you said—an attack of conscience."

Cheryl realized the chief was right. Bringing it here made no sense at all.

"I have to admit that I wondered more than once if you and Naomi were offtrack on this one," Chief Twitchell said. "I mean, anyone could have tried to make a homeless person look guilty to hide their own crimes. But like I said, what they stole didn't make sense. Then they dump the stuff here. And now this. I believe this is connected to you somehow. To Timothy being associated with you. Maybe you're gettin' too close."

"But the bear being here doesn't incriminate us," Cheryl said, trying to wrap her head around what the chief had said. "I mean, why put it in plain sight? It isn't as though they hid it and called you anonymously again, trying to make us look involved in the theft."

"Unless they thought you would keep it now that you know how valuable it is," the chief said.

"Maybe…" Cheryl said slowly. She knew Chief Twitchell was trying to find a reason the bear had been placed in the barn, but his assumption just didn't sound right to her. She felt as if the thief had returned the bear for a very different reason. Their barn was a safe place. He or she believed Cheryl would make sure it got back to the Fuszes. She couldn't prove it. It was just a gut feeling.

"Our place is out of town," Levi said. He sat down at the table. "Someone can obviously bring it here, put it in the barn, and leave without anyone knowing. We are the only people connected to the theft who live in the country."

"That's what I was just thinking. Since the Fuszes live in town, we were the best choice, right? They had to pick someone who knew what the bear was but wouldn't try to keep it."

"Right," Levi said. "The only other place out of town might have been my parents' house, but the road to their place is longer than ours. Easier to be seen. That makes sense, doesn't it?"

Cheryl nodded. "I guess it does, but here's another question. Why did they return it at all? Do most thieves return the things they steal?"

"That's the right question," Twitchell said. "Figure out the answer, and you'll have your thief." He put his hat back on. "I better get goin'. If I come up with anything I'll let you know. You do the same for me, okay?"

"Okay," Cheryl said. She followed him to the front door. "Chief, now that we have the bear, doesn't that knock the thefts down to a misdemeanor? Doesn't that mean you don't have to move Timothy to the county jail?"

"Unfortunately, some of the stolen items were expensive. Altogether, the value is just barely over a thousand dollars. That makes it a first-degree misdemeanor. It's not a felony, but it still carries a jail sentence of a hundred and eight days or a thousand-dollar fine. Maybe both."

Cheryl was disappointed. She desperately wanted Timothy to stay in Sugarcreek. The county jail would be much rougher for him.

"Chief, you are welcome to stay for supper," Levi said. "I promise we won't serve you cat food."

Chief Twitchell smiled. "I truly appreciate your invitation, but I need to get back. Delores has plans for tonight, and I promised to cover the phones."

Cheryl thought about asking why one of his officers couldn't do that, but she suspected the chief had given most of them time off for the holidays. Even though he had a tough exterior, the chief cared deeply about his officers, and they all seemed to respect him immensely.

"By the way, I've been checking around, asking about your angel," he said. "But nobody knows anything about her. I think your daughter imagined her. I don't think you have anything to worry about."

"I did not 'magine the angel!" Rebecca stepped into the living room and glared at the chief. "You stop askin' about her. You might scare her away!"

Rebecca burst into tears and ran out of the room, leaving Chief Twitchell looking so guilty, anyone watching might think he was personally hunting down and imprisoning angels out of spite.

Chapter Twenty-Eight

After Chief Twitchell left, Levi sat down with Rebecca, who was still upset. The chief had tried to apologize to her, but Rebecca wasn't having it. Evidently, in her mind he had the power to make the angel disappear.

Cheryl could tell Levi had his work cut out for him. Obviously, letting Rebecca think he didn't believe she'd seen an angel would be the wrong move. He wanted to comfort her, but he also needed to point out that her response to the chief wasn't appropriate. This was one time Cheryl was willing to let him take the lead. He cast several glances her way as if asking for help, but she just shrugged.

"Boo, the chief has been looking for your angel. He wouldn't do that if he didn't believe you saw something."

"But he doesn't believe she's a real angel, does he?" she asked, a tear sliding down her cheek.

Once again, Levi looked over at Cheryl. She sighed and joined them at the table. "Look, honey, what the chief believes doesn't make any difference. He's a good man, but that doesn't make him right about everything. No one knows the truth about everything."

"But I know about angels, Mama. They're in the Bible, you know."

Cheryl smiled. "Yes, I know about that."

"Do you and Daddy believe I saw the angel?"

This again. "Like we told you, we believe you think you saw an angel."

Rebecca slid down from her chair and ran from the room. Cheryl started to get up, but Levi stopped her.

"Let's leave her alone," he said. "She needs to think for a while. She knows she did not see a real angel."

"I disagree," Cheryl said softly, not wanting Rebecca to overhear her. "She's convinced the person she saw was an angel."

Just then Matthew crept quietly into the kitchen. "I hungry, Mama."

"Yes, honey. We'll eat in just a bit."

While Levi put him in his chair, Cheryl checked on the meat loaf and got some leftover mashed potatoes from the refrigerator. Then she rummaged in the freezer for a bag of green beans.

Rebecca returned to the kitchen. "See, Mama?" She held out her hand. There was something in it, but Cheryl couldn't tell what it was. It looked like a wadded-up piece of paper. She put out her hand, and Rebecca gave it to her.

"It got kinda smooshed up in my drawer," Rebecca said.

"Yeah, it looks smooshed up all right."

Cheryl looked at it more closely. What she saw surprised her. "It's origami," she said to Levi.

"No, Mama. It's an angel." Rebecca sounded surprised her mother didn't understand that the crumpled piece of paper was supposed to be a heavenly being.

As Cheryl carefully pulled the paper back into shape, it turned out Rebecca was right. It was an angel. Actually, it was very well done.

"The angel gave you this?" Cheryl asked.

Rebecca nodded. "Maybe I wasn't supposed to show you, but you already know about the angel, so I think it's all right."

There was no way Rebecca could have made something as intricate as this tiny angel. She had definitely met someone outside Monday night. It wasn't simply her imagination. This confirmed it.

"Why don't you wash your hands?" Levi suggested. "Supper is almost ready."

"Okay, Daddy." Rebecca headed toward the bathroom while Cheryl and Levi stared at each other.

"She definitely saw someone," Levi said.

"We need to try again to get her to describe her angel," Cheryl said. "It might help us figure out who it was."

"I agree," Levi said. "I will help you get supper on the table, and then we can discuss it while we eat."

"And, Levi, I'm wondering—how many dangerous people make origami angels for little girls?"

Levi shook his head. "I hear what you are saying, but I still do not like someone advising our child not to tell us that she talked to them."

Cheryl didn't respond, but he was right. That upset her too.

Levi heated up the green beans and mashed potatoes while Cheryl got the meat loaf out of the oven and fixed the drinks. Ten minutes later they were eating. Thankfully, Rebecca and Matthew liked meat loaf. Cheryl had made a few adjustments for them. The green peppers and onions had to be diced smaller and more ketchup poured on top, but they both ate it now. Levi loved meat loaf the way she made it.

After they were a few bites into their meal, Cheryl said, "Hey, Boo, tell us what your angel looked like. I've never seen one. I'd really like to know more about her."

Rebecca finished swallowing a mouthful of mashed potatoes. "She was all white. White hair, white clothes. And she shined."

"She shined?" Levi repeated. "Why did she shine? Did she have lights inside of her?"

Rebecca looked puzzled for a moment. "You told me that the love of God shines from inside us, Daddy," she said.

"Ja, I did." Levi took a deep breath and let it out slowly. Obviously, he was changing tactics. "And was the light coming out of her mouth? Her eyes?" He grinned at Rebecca. "Her belly button?"

Rebecca and Matthew both laughed. Cheryl was fairly certain Matthew was just laughing at Levi saying "belly button."

"No, Daddy. I couldn't see her belly button. An angel doesn't show people her belly button. You made Matthew stop doing that."

"Ja, I remember," Levi said. Cheryl could tell he was trying hard not to laugh.

"I don't know where the light came from. It was all over her."

Cheryl suddenly realized something. "Boo, was the angel standing in front of the barn?"

Rebecca nodded vigorously. "Yes. In front of the barn."

Cheryl realized the floodlight from the barn must have been behind the angel, making her look as though she was shining. She looked at Levi and could tell he'd figured out the same thing. At least that mystery was solved.

Cheryl decided it was time to move away from talking about the angel and onto something else. She brought up Christmas Day and that Oma and Opa were coming over as well as their aunts and uncles. Rebecca started to bring up her Christmas list again, but Levi steered her away from that and onto the story of Jesus in the manger. That took them through supper and right up to baths and bed.

While Levi bathed the children, Cheryl cleaned up the kitchen and put the food away. She stared out the kitchen window at the darkened dawdy haus. Tomorrow was Thursday. They were running out of time. Timothy was being sent to the county jail on Friday, and they still had no idea who had framed him. She wasn't sure they were going to figure it out in time.

Chapter Twenty-Nine

The next morning Cheryl cleaned up the breakfast dishes and straightened the house. Levi was going to the church to finish repairing the nativity and to get it set up. The people acting the roles would do so Friday night through Sunday night. She didn't envy them. It was supposed to be really cold. She wasn't sure they would even be able to pull off their first night. The snowstorm they'd been waiting for was moving in tonight, and although weather forecasters kept changing the totals, it was supposed to dump quite a bit of snow in Ohio.

Cheryl looked up Kasey's Kountry Kupboard online and found pictures of Kasey and Dallas. She planned to show them to Timothy. She wanted to know if he recognized either of them. She was also able to find an old newspaper that had an announcement about the Fuszes' fiftieth wedding anniversary. Cheryl had kept the paper because it had an ad for the Swiss Miss. Thankfully, cutting out the announcement didn't affect the ad.

Cheryl had called the church to see if the volunteer committees were meeting this morning. She wanted Levi to take Rebecca and Matthew with him. He might not be part of a committee, but he certainly was a volunteer. After finding out that they were and that there would be childcare, she checked to see if they had room for Rebecca and Matthew. She was assured that they would be welcome, which was great since Naomi was coming over to talk about Timothy, and Cheryl didn't want a lot of interruptions.

At first Levi said he didn't think he could take them since he had to go to the jail, but Cheryl convinced him that he could drop the children off at the church before going to the jail. After that, he could work on the nativity. He wasn't crazy about doing it that way, but he finally agreed after Cheryl reminded him that they only had today to find a way to keep Timothy from being transferred out of town. She gave him the newspaper clipping and the pictures she'd printed from Kasey's website. She also gave him the gifts she'd bought for the needy child at church. He promised to drop them off with the pastor's secretary, who was coordinating the collection of the items.

Levi and the children had been gone about ten minutes when Naomi arrived in her buggy. She and Cheryl took Sugar and Spice into the barn so they would keep warm while the women visited.

"Coffee?" Cheryl asked when they were back inside.

"Ja, please," Naomi said as she took off her cloak and hung it on the coatrack.

"And how about some coffeecake? Not as good as yours, I'm sure."

"Ach, Cheryl. You are a wonderful cook. You must believe more in yourself."

"But wouldn't that be a lack of humility?" Cheryl asked, grinning.

Naomi laughed. "You are trying to put words in my mouth. Real humility is telling the truth. And you are a very good cook."

"Hmm. I think you just turned that around on me somehow."

Naomi smiled. "I will never admit it though."

It was Cheryl's turn to laugh. She put their cups and the slices of cake on a tray and carried it into the living room to the coffee table. While they ate, Cheryl told Naomi about the night before.

"So the bear just turned up in your barn?" Naomi asked, looking surprised. "That is very strange."

"Extremely. I called the Fuszes this morning and told them about the bear. I promised to take it to them tomorrow. They sounded very happy about it."

"I believe that lets them off the hook," Naomi said. "If they were trying to get the insurance money, they would not be happy about the bear turning up." She frowned. "As happy as I am about the recovered bear, I am very concerned about it suddenly showing up in your barn. This means someone snuck onto your property, twice now. Was your barn not locked?"

Cheryl shook her head. "We've never felt as if we needed to lock it, but I guess we need to rethink that."

Naomi nodded. "We do not leave our barn locked either, but we can easily see it from the house. We also have never felt the need."

"I guess thieves are everywhere. Even in Sugarcreek. It isn't like we've never seen dishonest people before."

"That is very true," Naomi said. "But to bring the bear back. I may be wrong, but this looks like remorse."

Cheryl took another sip of coffee. "It might be. It's strange, isn't it? I keep asking myself why the bear wasn't with the other stolen items hidden in our dawdy haus. That's why I suspected the Fuszes."

"I might wonder if Herschel or Nettie put the bear out there because they regretted taking it, but they're both elderly and not in the best health." Naomi shook her head. "No, I can't see either one of them traipsing around outside and sneaking into your barn at night."

Cheryl agreed. "You're right. It would be almost impossible for them to do that. Besides," she said, "I don't want to be mistrustful of everyone. That doesn't bring peace."

"I agree," Naomi said. "But I do not think we are making any progress when it comes to Timothy. We have not excluded anyone from our list, except Herschel and Nettie."

"I know. And Timothy will be sent to the county jail tomorrow."

"But Chief Twitchell knows now that Timothy did not take the bear," Naomi said. "Does this not help Timothy's cause?"

"Yes, it does. The chief knows Timothy had nothing to do with the bear. But that doesn't let him off the hook when it comes to the other thefts. He thinks Timothy is innocent, but he has to send him on unless he can prove he didn't do it."

"And he is wanting our help, ain't so? I must admit that I am unsure we are going to be able to provide it." Naomi took a sip of her coffee. "We are assuming Timothy is being accused falsely. And we are assuming the person doing this has something against him. Something about Timothy that made them pick him out. But what if it is someone else? Someone who has lived in Sugarcreek for many years and simply needed to make someone else look guilty? A homeless man is an easy target."

Cheryl shook her head. "We've been over this, Naomi. The items weren't worth much. It was difficult for whoever did this to bring them here and hide them. Then the anonymous phone call by someone who knew his full name. And that the stolen items were in the dawdy haus where he was staying. All those facts brought us to our conclusion. No, I'm sticking with my original suspicions. This isn't just someone trying to pin the thefts on some homeless guy. Timothy is a target. We need to find out why. I think if we do that, we'll get the answers we need."

"If you say so…"

Cheryl could tell something was bothering Naomi. Why was she rehashing conclusions they'd already rejected?

"Is everything okay?" Cheryl asked.

"I am sorry, Cheryl. I cannot stop thinking about Sarah. I sent her a letter telling her how much we love her. I wrote about you and Levi, how we are doing so well even though Levi left our faith. That we want to mend fences with her. But the letter was returned. It seems the last address I had for them is no longer correct. They have moved, and I have no idea where they are now."

"Maybe they just bought another house in Canton."

"That may be true, but how will I ever find them? Sarah obviously does not want me to know their location or she would have sent me her new address. I have written to her before. She did not respond, but at least the letters were not returned."

"She'll come around, Naomi. I just know it. You have to have faith."

"I know you are right. I am sorry to burden you with this."

Cheryl shook her head. "You are never a burden to me. You are one of my greatest blessings."

Naomi nodded. "As are you to me." She straightened in her chair. "Now, back to our young friend. We must connect someone else to the thefts for the chief to drop the charges and keep Timothy here, ain't so?"

"Exactly," Cheryl said. "Let's recap. We're taking the Fuszes off the list, because, as you said, they just don't seem like the type of people to try to get the insurance money in a dishonest way. Yes, they insured the bear for more than it's worth, but I think that has to do with replacement value. It's still quite a bit more than the appraisal I received, but the appraiser admitted that without seeing the bear, she could only guess. And what you said about it being difficult for them to drop the bear off in our barn makes it even less likely that they're involved."

"All right."

"Before we move forward, I've learned something new about Rebecca's angel." She told Naomi about her and Levi's conversation with Rebecca. Then she showed Naomi the origami figure and repeated Rebecca's description of the angel.

"So she actually saw a woman dressed in white, highlighted by the floodlight?"

Cheryl took a sip of her coffee. "Seems so. Not quite as angelic as we thought. And I don't quite understand what kind of an angel does origami."

"No, I do not either. But Cheryl, what kind of person wears all white? I mean, some Amish women wear white dresses, but not out in the cold. She would wear a cloak. And Rebecca would recognize an Amish woman by her kapp."

"You're right. She said the angel had white hair." She frowned. "Maybe I should ask her if her angel was Amish. It never occurred to me."

Naomi put her hand over her mouth as she laughed. "So there was an Amish woman dressed in white outside your barn the other night who makes origami angels and doesn't wear a coat in the winter?"

"Well, when you say it like that—"

"I suppose it would not be wrong to ask, but I do not know anyone like that."

Cheryl took another sip of coffee. "Let's assume the angel isn't Amish. I know the timing is odd, the angel showing up at about the same time as the robberies, but I still think Kasey and Dallas are the ones behind this."

"But why?" Naomi asked. "You suspected them of taking the bear, but it has been returned. Why would they steal the other things? And what is their motive? What do they have to do with Timothy?"

"Levi is going by the jail this morning. He's going to show Timothy pictures of Kasey and Dallas that I printed from the store's website and see if he recognizes them."

"That should be helpful, but I still am not sure these people would return the bear. Why not just hide it so no one will find out they took it?"

Cheryl leaned back on the couch and crossed her arms. She'd been so sure it was either Kasey or Dallas. But Naomi was right. Why would they take a chance on bringing the bear here, knowing they might be seen? It didn't make sense. Neither one of them seemed to be the kind of person who would have an attack of conscience.

"I believe the bear's appearance changes everything," Naomi said. "We need to rethink this. You said the thefts had something to do with Timothy. But why would Kasey want to hurt Timothy? He said he didn't know anyone in Sugarcreek. And the Fuszes don't know him either. I do not think our suspects look guilty. What are we missing?"

Cheryl sat silently, trying to figure out what any of their suspects had to do with Timothy. The answer was…nothing. It was as if their entire list had just crashed and burned. And unless Timothy recognized Kasey or Dallas, or they could figure out who had returned the bear, there was no chance they would be able to solve this mystery in time to help Timothy.

CHAPTER THIRTY

Cheryl and Naomi talked a while longer, trying to make sense of the thefts and their relation to Timothy, but they couldn't come up with a scenario they felt comfortable with. While they were talking, Cheryl's phone rang. It was Levi, who told her that Timothy claimed he had never seen Kasey, Dallas, or the Fuszes before.

After she hung up, Cheryl shared Levi's news with Naomi. Although Cheryl had wanted Kasey to be guilty, with Levi's news and not being able to connect the bear to the unpleasant woman, she had to take her off their list too, along with Dallas. Their list of suspects had shrunk to almost zero.

"Maybe we need to figure out who the angel is," she told Naomi. "In the end, she's the most suspicious. Showing up on our property—and telling Rebecca not to tell us she talked to her."

"But how can we discover her identity?" Naomi asked. "Unless she comes back and you are able to catch her, we cannot prove she is behind this plan to make Timothy look guilty. And we have no proof that she knows Timothy either. So what is her motive?"

Frankly, Cheryl was getting a little tired of hearing about angels. An angel paying off Mamie Abernathy's mortgage. An angel paying for Grimmy's surgery. Pastor Brotton mentioning that Rosalind Price's trip to see her mother might happen. Then there was the angel outside their barn. Cheryl was thrilled about all the needs that were being met at the church. But who was really behind it? What was going on?

She wanted to call Pastor Brotton and ask the identity of the person providing help to all the people in need in their church, but trying to explain that it might have something to do with an angel her five-year-old daughter saw by their barn sounded ridiculous. Besides, it really wasn't any of her business. Pastor Brotton wouldn't tell her who it was anyway.

"I wish we could find out who called the police and told them about the stolen items hidden in the dawdy haus," Naomi said. "It has to be the person we are looking for. But the police were not able to figure out where the call came from?"

"No. It wasn't traceable. The chief said they couldn't even tell if it was a man or a woman. The person disguised their voice. We just know that whoever called knew Timothy's full name. No one else I've talked to had that information. The call just doesn't help us at all."

By the time Naomi left to go home, they'd admitted to each other that there was nothing they could do to stop Timothy from being transferred the next day. That meant he would have to spend Christmas Day in the county jail. Cheryl felt awful about it but had no idea how she could help at this point. Unless the chief could pull off some kind of miracle and find a way to drop the charges, there was really nothing anyone could do.

Cheryl took the rest of the morning and afternoon to clean the house, including Matthew's and Rebecca's rooms. It was much easier to straighten their bedrooms when they weren't in them pulling out toys to play with. She was also able to wrap some gifts and put them under the tree. It really was a beautiful tree. She'd already put up some of their other decorations. She'd added some things to the fireplace mantel, but it didn't look the same without her nativity set.

It was almost five o'clock when she heard Levi's truck pull into the driveway. She'd just put the vacuum cleaner away, so his timing was perfect. Beau, who hated it when she vacuumed, slid out from underneath the couch. He gave her a look that said, "Are you finished with that evil device?" She couldn't help but laugh at him.

It didn't take long for the quiet inside the house to be broken. As soon as the front door opened Cheryl heard Rebecca calling out, "Mama, Mama, Mama…"

Beau jumped on top of the couch and lay down in his favorite spot. She could have sworn he rolled his eyes.

Cheryl left the kitchen and went into the living room. Rebecca and Matthew struggled to get out of their coats, hats, and mittens. Levi was trying to help Matthew get his arms out of his coat sleeves while Rebecca had just pulled her coat over her head, ignoring the buttons altogether.

"Mama, Mama, Mama," she began again.

Cheryl held her arms out, and Rebecca ran to her. "What is it, Boo?" she asked.

"Big, big storm comin'. Pastor Brotton said there might not be any 'tivity tomorrow night."

Cheryl looked over at Levi, who nodded. "We were hoping the storm would dissipate, but it seems it has only grown in strength. I am going out to take care of the horses before it hits."

"What about Bun Bun?" Rebecca asked.

"I will feed him this time," Levi said.

"But will he be okay, Daddy? What about the big storm?"

"He will be fine, honey. I will make sure he is nice and warm. He will not even know it is snowing."

Rebecca studied her father for a moment but finally seemed to decide he could be trusted with her precious rabbit.

"Okay, Daddy. Will you tell Bun Bun I love him?"

Levi sighed and grinned at Cheryl. "Ja, I will tell him."

Cheryl knew her husband would keep his word. Telling the truth was very important to him.

"I am sorry Timothy did not recognize anyone, Cheryl. It seems we have not found anything that will exonerate him. He is aware of this and is prepared to be transferred."

"Maybe the storm will keep that from happening."

Levi shrugged. "It is possible. Perhaps that will allow the chief to let him stay over the weekend."

"And maybe he could come here for Christmas?"

"Maybe. We will have to see. I cannot guarantee that the chief would allow it, but I suspect that if it is possible, he will try to make it happen."

"I think you're right."

Levi turned and went out the front door. Cheryl found her phone and brought up the latest weather report. Levi was right.

This promised to be a major storm, with over a foot of snow. She looked out the window and saw that flakes were already beginning to fall. She wasn't as concerned about the accumulation as she was about the wind. Out here where they lived, power outages happened frequently. Thankfully, Levi had purchased a generator that would automatically turn on if the electricity went out. It had proven to be one of the best things they'd ever bought.

Rebecca let her know that Levi had bought them burgers for lunch. She loved cheeseburgers and the small toys the fast-food restaurant placed in their meals.

"I chicken," Matthew said.

"You got the chicken nuggets?" Cheryl asked with a smile.

He nodded happily and walked over to where Beau was still curled up on the couch. "Hi, Beau." He ran his hand lightly over the cat's back.

"Good job, Matthew," Cheryl said. "Do you hear how happy Beau is when you pet him gently?"

Beau's purring was loud enough for all of them to hear. Matthew beamed with joy. "Beau good kitty," he said softly.

"Yes, he is a good kitty." Cheryl smiled at her children. "How about some hot chocolate?"

"Yes, please, Mama," Rebecca said.

"Yes, peas," Matthew echoed.

With the snow falling, the fire crackling in the fireplace, and the promise of a cozy evening at home, Cheryl should have felt happy.

But she couldn't shake the picture of Timothy sitting all alone in his holding cell wondering what was going to become of him.

CHAPTER THIRTY-ONE

As promised, the snow continued to pile up. Levi played games with the kids in the living room while Cheryl prepared supper. Everyone in the family really enjoyed taco casserole. It felt like the perfect meal on a snowy evening.

After supper, she cleaned up the kitchen while Levi gave Rebecca and Matthew their baths. They'd decided to watch *It's a Wonderful Life*, Cheryl's favorite Christmas movie. When everyone was ready, they took their places in the living room. Levi had just added another log to the fire when a large gust of wind shook the house. The electricity flickered and went out. Matthew started to cry, but seconds later the generator kicked in and the electricity was restored. A few minutes later they were watching the movie. It wasn't long before Rebecca and Matthew were both asleep. Cheryl had expected this result. Although Rebecca was old enough to enjoy the movie, it was a little late for her. Cheryl and Levi got them both in bed and then headed back into the living room.

"How about a bowl of popcorn?" Cheryl asked.

Levi nodded. "Sounds perfect. Can I help?"

"Nah, you worked hard at the church today," Cheryl said. "You never said how it went. Were you able to repair the stable enough for the church to use it?"

Levi sighed. "The best I can say is that as long as the wind doesn't blow like it did earlier, we should be able to make it one more year. But that is not a guarantee."

"I guess we better pray that Rebecca's angel shows up and holds things together."

"That would be helpful."

Cheryl had just taken the bag out of the microwave and put the butter in to melt when she heard a loud noise that shook the house. She recognized it immediately. Thunder snow. It rarely happened, but it seemed tonight they were going to experience the phenomenon.

Matthew cried out, and Rebecca yelled, "Mama! Mama!"

Cheryl had just reached up to turn off the microwave so she could go to her children when she noticed Beau run into the kitchen and crouch under the table. The thunder had frightened him too. A moment later Rebecca came running into the kitchen.

"Mama, the house was shaking!" she said.

"Honey, it's okay. It's just thunder. Remember when we talked about thunder?" She could hear Levi in the living room trying to calm Matthew down.

"Bun Bun must be so scared," Rebecca said, a tear slipping down her face. "I need to go out and help him. He might be crying."

"No, Boo. Not right now. Let's wait until the thunder stops. Then we'll check on him and the horses."

Just then, another loud peal of thunder shook the house. This time Rebecca screamed. Cheryl forgot about the popcorn and leaned down to pick her up. Then she carried her into the living room where Levi was still trying to assure Matthew that everything was all right. It took several minutes to calm them down. Thankfully, there were no more cracks of thunder.

Cheryl finished making the popcorn while Levi got the kids settled on the sofa so they could restart the movie. It was a nice evening, even though Rebecca kept bringing up Bun Bun. At one point, Levi stopped the movie and promised her that he would check on the rabbit and the horses in the morning. The snow was supposed to continue through the night but stop not long after sunrise. Although Cheryl was pretty sure Rebecca wasn't completely satisfied with her father's response, at least she finally settled down. As expected, Matthew fell asleep again not long after Levi restarted the movie. Levi carried him to bed. Surprisingly, Rebecca stayed awake until the end.

When the movie was over, Cheryl told Rebecca it was time for bed. She didn't argue and went into her bedroom and closed the door.

"I think she's still mad at us because we refused to check on Bun Bun and the horses tonight," Cheryl told Levi.

"I suspect you are right," he said. "But with the wind piling up the snow, it would not be wise for me to venture out. I'm certain the animals are all right. They are very adaptable." He grinned at her. "Me? Not so much."

She smiled at him. "I think you're very adaptable. You've gone from living Amish to watching a movie on TV with your family."

"This is true, but I am still learning. However, I draw the line at reality TV."

Cheryl laughed. "But Levi, some of it is so good. Like *The Amazing Race*. That's even educational at times."

He snorted. "Ja, you showed me part of that show. The couple had to eat cheese with maggots in it. No thank you. I will stick with your food if you do not mind."

"I hope you think it's a step above maggots."

"Of course I do. At least one step."

Cheryl laughed and hit him with a couch pillow.

Levi stood up and yawned. "Bedtime for me." He started picking up the empty popcorn bowls to take into the kitchen. "Where is Beau? He usually joins us on the couch when we watch TV."

Cheryl had wondered about that too but had assumed he was somewhere nearby. She got up from the couch and began calling softly to him. She checked some of his usual places without finding him. Finally, she heard his meow and discovered him in the bedroom, under the bed.

"Oh, Beau," she said to him. "I'm so sorry. Did the thunder scare you?"

She knew he didn't like thunder, but usually he would just want to snuggle with her until it passed. She had no idea why he'd escaped to the bedroom, but she finally coaxed him out. Then she picked him up and carried him into the kitchen, where Levi was loading the dishwasher.

"He was hiding under our bed," she told him. "I guess the thunder scared him and he needed a quiet place to decompress." She gave Beau a hug. "I feel the same way sometimes, Beau." She put him down and went to the pantry, where she found a can of tuna. Beau knew what was happening as soon as she opened the can. "How about a special treat, sweetie?" She put some tuna in his bowl, and he ran over to it, purring so loudly she and Levi laughed.

Levi started the dishwasher and turned to face her. "I was a little concerned about the thunder too. I think I deserve a special treat. Do we have any cheesecake left?"

"Yes, we do. But it's for after supper tomorrow. You stay out of it."

Levi let out a big, dramatic sigh. "See, Beau," he said, addressing the cat, "she dotes on you and ignores me. Be careful. This could happen to you too someday."

"You're ridiculous," Cheryl said, grinning. "We need to get some sleep. We're going to have a lot of snow to shovel tomorrow."

"You are right about that."

Cheryl turned off the light in the kitchen, and she and Levi headed to bed. Beau followed behind them, and before long they were all asleep.

Rebecca waited until she was sure Mama and Daddy were asleep. Then she tiptoed downstairs and put on her coat and the boots Mama made her wear outside when it snowed. She pulled up the hood on her coat and waited a little bit to make sure no one had heard her. She could hear Daddy snoring upstairs. Then she slowly walked into the kitchen. She had to make sure Bun Bun was okay. That he wasn't scared. He was just a baby and needed her. She wasn't sure why Mama and Daddy had told her she couldn't go outside, but she knew she had to help him.

She opened the door and then tried to open the storm door, but it wouldn't move. Rebecca pushed and pushed against it until she got it open a little bit. She squeezed through and finally got out onto the porch. It was very cold and snowy. The wind blew the snow into her face. For just a minute she wondered if she should go back, but if she did, it meant she wasn't a good mama to her bunny. She had to keep going.

Rebecca looked for the light from the barn as she trudged through the snow. She thought she saw it and kept walking, but after a while she started getting tired. She finally gave up and wanted to go back inside the house. She was so cold and so tired. All she wanted to do was get into her warm bed. She was still worried about Bun Bun and felt bad that she couldn't help him.

After trying to find her house she realized she was lost and started to cry. She called for her mama and daddy until she couldn't talk anymore. She was so cold. She saw a tree nearby and went over to it. Then she sat down and prayed that God would send her angel to save her.

CHAPTER THIRTY-TWO

Cheryl had been asleep for a while when she heard someone call her name. At first, she thought she was dreaming. But when she heard the voice a second time, she sat up in bed. Was it Levi? She reached out a hand and felt for him beside her. He was asleep and snoring lightly. It wasn't him. It had to be one of the kids.

She got out of bed and made her way to Matthew's room. He too was sound asleep. Then she went into Rebecca's room. At first Cheryl thought her little girl was under the covers, but she quickly realized that the only thing under the bedspread was a pillow. It looked like Rebecca had tried to make her bed. But where was she?

Cheryl checked the bathroom. She wasn't there. Then she went into the living room. No Rebecca.

By the time she reached the kitchen she was beginning to panic. Where could she be? It was then that she noticed the back door was open. She knew instantly what had happened. Rebecca had been worried about Bun Bun. She'd gone out to make sure he was okay even though her father had told her he would check on him in the morning. Cheryl pushed the storm door farther open. It took all the strength she had. Snow had piled up against the door, and it felt as if the wind was fighting to keep it shut. Cheryl couldn't even see the bottom of the steps. A sense of urgency filled her. Rebecca was in trouble and needed help—now.

Cheryl found her phone and dialed 911 as she ran to the bedroom and woke Levi up. She explained to the 911 operator where they were and that their five-year-old daughter was out in the blizzard.

By this time Levi was awake and listening to what she was telling the operator. "If we find her before you get here, I'll call you back," Cheryl told the dispatcher.

"No, ma'am," the woman said. "You need to stay on the line with me until help arrives. I would advise you not to go out in this storm," she warned. "I'll dispatch emergency response. They're trained to search for missing children—even in weather like this."

"But where are they located?" Cheryl asked. "We're in Sugarcreek."

"Yes, ma'am. I realize that. Your local fire department personnel are trained in emergency rescue. I realize it's a volunteer station, but they receive the same training every fire department gets."

By this time Levi was dressed and pulling on his boots.

"The 911 operator said we shouldn't go out in this," she told him, covering the mouthpiece of her phone. "That we should wait for the fire department to get here."

"Did she? I have no plan to leave our daughter out there alone in this blizzard."

Cheryl knew that was what he would say, but she was relieved to hear it. She hurried into the living room, grabbed her coat from the coatrack, and put it on, all the while hanging on to her phone. Levi was just coming out of the bedroom and saw her.

"No, Cheryl. Absolutely not. You must stay here with Matthew. What if something happens—"

"Nothing is going to happen," she told him. Suddenly something filled her. An assurance. Faith that everything would be okay. "Levi, someone woke me up. Called my name twice. God is watching over Rebecca. I just know it."

"I believe you, Cheryl. But I still must look for her. I cannot sit in the house and wait. Gott will watch over me as well. Pray for us." He leaned over and kissed her cheek. "I will bring her home. I promise."

Cheryl walked him to the back door and hugged him before he made his way off the porch and into the blizzard, a flashlight in his hand. She walked farther out onto the porch, turned on the light, and held onto the handrail. The wind screamed at her. It felt like all the elements were against them. But if she had ever been sure of anything in her life, she was sure of this. God would bring Rebecca home safely.

As she stood there, something streaked past her, making her yell out in surprise. It was Beau. Before she could stop him, he ran out into the storm. Tears filled her eyes. Why would he do that? He hated snow and cold. What was he thinking?

"Bring all three of them home to me, God," she prayed. "My beloved little girl, my wonderful husband, and my sweet Beau. I trust You to watch over them."

Rebecca wasn't cold anymore, but she was sleepy. She wished she was in her bed, warm and safe. Maybe if she went to sleep, when she woke up, she would be back in her room.

She'd just closed her eyes when she heard someone call her name. Rebecca smiled. She knew she would come. Her angel was here. She reached out for her, and the angel sat down next to her, wrapping her wings around her. Rebecca put her head on the angel's chest and closed her eyes.

Cheryl had gone inside to check on Matthew several times. He was still sound asleep. She stayed on the phone with the dispatcher and tried to ignore how long Levi had been gone. Why wasn't he back yet? Rebecca couldn't have gone far. Her little legs should have kept her close by.

She stood on the back porch again and peered into the snow. She'd searched for another flashlight and found one, but it wasn't as powerful as Levi's. She pointed it at the snow anyway, hoping she could see Levi returning. Several times she thought she saw something. Was certain it was Levi, but each time it was just the snow creating shapes that resembled people. Or maybe that was just what she wanted to see.

She kept reminding herself of the peace she'd felt earlier. Of the assurance she had that God had everything under control. As the minutes ticked by, she had to fight harder and harder to hold on to that thought. She had just come to the conclusion that she had to go out there and find her family when once again she thought she saw shapes in the snow.

From somewhere in the distance, the whine of an emergency vehicle became louder and louder. Cheryl had just ended the call with the dispatcher when in front of her the snow parted. Out of the darkness stepped someone dressed all in white. Was it an angel?

As the figure got closer, she realized Levi was there also, Rebecca in his arms. Beau ran out from behind them. With tears falling down her frozen cheeks, Cheryl thanked God for answering her prayers. She held the door open for her family to enter—as well as the angel that helped bring Rebecca home.

CHAPTER THIRTY-THREE

After drying Rebecca off, Cheryl let one of the firefighters check her over.

"She seems fine," he told her. "I don't see any signs of frostbite. This is one lucky little lady."

Cheryl nodded, knowing that luck had nothing to do with it. "Thank you so much for coming out," she told the man. "We really appreciate it."

"We're just grateful everyone found their way home safely."

Beau's soft snoring from the other end of the couch made Cheryl want to cry. She still couldn't understand why he'd run out into the storm.

"Can we take you back to your vehicle?" the man asked Rebecca's angel.

"No, thank you. It's actually parked in the driveway," Judith said. "It's a miracle I saw this child from the road. It was her dark coat that made me look again." She pointed toward her white coat that was drying in front of the fire. "I thank God I didn't get lost in that storm. That old coat would have blended in with the snow, and no one could have seen me." She blinked away tears. "It was a gift from my husband. He thought it was beautiful. Since he passed away, I haven't been able to get rid of it. It reminds me of him."

"Well, according to my daughter it makes you look like an angel," Cheryl said with a smile.

Judith laughed. "Now, that's something no one's ever said to me before."

"We need to get going," the man from the fire department said. "The wind has died down some. It should be a lot easier to find our way back. It was tough going getting here—and that's in a big truck." He shook his head. "I'm still not sure how all of you made it through this unscathed, but I'd take it as a really wonderful Christmas gift."

"We know who brought us home," Levi said softly.

"Wouldn't you and your crew like a cup of coffee before you go?" Cheryl asked. "I just made a pot."

The man smiled. "Thanks, but we have a large thermos in the truck. We appreciate it though."

Levi turned on the front porch light, and the men headed outside. Cheryl heard them start their engine. The sound faded as they drove away.

"I need to put this little girl to bed," Levi said. "She's already asleep." He picked Rebecca up from the chair where she was still wrapped up in the towel Cheryl had used to dry her off.

"Be sure to change her clothes," Cheryl said.

Levi shook his head. "I did not plan to put her into bed wearing these wet things."

"I know, honey. I'm sorry. I just…" Cheryl wiped away a tear that snaked down her cheek. "I'm so glad you found her," she said, her voice breaking.

Levi got a strange look on his face. "I'm not sure who found who." He looked at Judith. "I think we both had another angel out there, ain't so?"

"Yes, I believe you're right," she said with a smile.

After Levi left the room, Cheryl frowned at Judith. "I'm sorry, I don't understand. There's another angel? Besides you?"

"Oh, my dear. I'm not an angel. Trust me. I met your daughter the night I brought some food over for Timothy. I probably shouldn't have told her to keep me a secret. When I thought about it later, I realized it was the wrong thing to do. I'm sorry if I caused you any worry. You see, I've been doing some things that…well, I'd like to keep quiet."

"I don't understand," Cheryl said. "What do you mean?"

Judith smiled. "I'll make you a deal. You pour me a big cup of that coffee you just made, and I'll fill you in. Does that sound fair to you?"

"Yes, it does. I could use some coffee too."

By the time Cheryl had poured three cups and carried them into the living room, Levi had returned. Judith sat in a chair while Cheryl, Levi, and Beau took up the couch. Cheryl stroked Beau. She was so grateful he'd made it back. She'd felt confident Rebecca would come home safely, but she hadn't been so sure about Beau.

Judith took a few sips before putting her mug on the coffee table. "I guess I'll start from the beginning. My nephew, Jordan, lost his father, my husband's youngest brother, when he was young, and his mother had emotional problems. We tried to fill in the best we could. Be the parents he didn't have. We became very close, almost as if he were our own son.

"About three years ago he met a girl from Sugarcreek who was visiting family in our town. She and Jordan fell madly in love and ended up getting married. He moved here after her father offered him a job at a local cheese factory that he owns."

"We know the owner," Cheryl said. "And I think I know the young man you mean. Very nice."

"Yes, he is. He and his wife purchased some land out here that was originally meant for farming, but they have no intention of venturing into that. They built a large house for lots of children, so for now there's plenty of room for visitors like me."

"That's wonderful."

"Yes, it is." Judith sighed. "I didn't plan to travel to Sugarcreek in the winter, but all my children have plans with in-laws for Christmas, and so I decided it was a good time to see Jordan and Abby. They were expecting their first child any day now, and I was hoping I could make things a little easier for Abby while I'm here."

"That makes sense," Cheryl said. She looked over at Levi. "I met Judith at church on Tuesday morning when I attended the Benevolence Committee meeting."

Judith smiled. "And now to keep my side of the bargain and tell you my secret. You see, my husband was a wonderful and very frugal man. He was also a brilliant man. He worked as an engineer for a technology company. He was paid a high salary, and in his spare time he designed computer programs. I didn't know about this until after he died." She paused. "He was old-fashioned. Believed that the husband should pay the bills and control the money. It wasn't because he looked down on me in any way. He truly believed it was his job to take care of me and make sure I was happy."

Judith took another sip of her coffee. "Not only did I discover that we were rich—very rich—I also found out that he had a large life insurance policy. I'll just say this. I will never have to worry about finances for the rest of my life. In fact, there's no way I could possibly spend it all, so I decided to use some of the money to help people."

Cheryl had picked up her mug when what Judith said suddenly hit her. "You brought food for Timothy. And you're the one who paid for Grimmy's surgery."

"Yes, and I am making sure that the woman who needs to visit her mother gets to go. I was able to hire a private plane to fly her back and forth."

Cheryl's mouth dropped open. "Don't tell me you're also the one who paid off Mamie Abernathy's loan so she can stay in her house?"

Judith smiled. "I must ask you to keep all of this to yourself. I need the freedom to help where it's needed without being inundated by people asking for a handout. Can you understand that?"

"Yes, I can. Mum's the word."

"You say you are not an angel," Levi said, "but I think you are mistaken. You are certainly an angel to some very good people who were in need."

"I appreciate that. You know when people say that they're ones who are blessed when they're able to help people?"

Cheryl nodded.

"I used to think that was some kind of false humility. But I'm finding out they're telling the truth." Her eyes grew shiny. "Since my husband died, this is the happiest I've been. Using our money to help people has given me back my joy."

"You said earlier that there was another angel out in the storm. Someone else who helped you find Rebecca?"

"Yes," Levi said. "First I heard Judith calling out for help, but it was so hard to see. I couldn't find her. Suddenly, Beau showed up in front of me, rubbing against my leg. He led me to them. And he also helped us find our way home. He stayed in front of us the entire time. It was as if…"

"He knew exactly what he was doing," Judith finished for him. "And you all came just in time. I saw Rebecca under a tree close to the road."

Cheryl felt a shiver run down her spine. "She must have gotten turned around in the storm and didn't know which way to go to the barn."

"Yes," Judith said. "She told me that she was worried about her bunny. At first I sat with her and tried to keep her warm. But after a few minutes, I began to realize that I needed to get her inside, so I picked her up and began to carry her. I'm afraid I'm not as strong as I was when I was younger. I'm not sure how much farther I could have held on to her. I kept calling out for help, and then your husband and your beautiful Beau showed up. Without this special cat, I'm not sure we would have made it back."

"Yes, he really is special," Cheryl said, her voice choked. "I think he may get some more tuna tonight."

Could he have really understood that Rebecca was in trouble? And did he actually lead all of them home? She'd heard of animals doing some incredible things, but this was hard to believe. She finally decided that God was a God of miracles, and she wouldn't try to second-guess His grace and mercy. If He wanted to use Beau to save their precious daughter, who was she to argue?

Chapter Thirty-Four

Levi got up from the couch. "I can never thank you enough for helping us," he said to Judith. "Perhaps you can come for supper sometime soon. But I must admit, I need to get some sleep. I will say good night now."

"Good night, Levi," Judith said. "It would be my pleasure to have supper with your lovely family one of these days. Thank you."

Levi left the room. Cheryl was tired too, but she could tell it would be hard to sleep now. She realized that Judith was older than she was and that she probably needed to get home.

"Do you want Levi or me to drive you home?" she asked. "You must be exhausted."

"Thank you, but I'll be fine. It's really not that far. Besides, your coffee will keep me awake for a while."

Cheryl frowned. "Do you mind if I ask why you were out so late…and in a snowstorm?"

"Jordan and Abby were expecting their first baby a few weeks from now, but Abby went into labor earlier today. I drove them to the hospital because my truck has four-wheel-drive. They had a bag packed, but in the rush to get to the hospital, Jordan forgot to load it. I told them I'd get it and bring it to the hospital. I thought I could get back before the storm got really bad." She laughed. "I was wrong. But the truth is, I think I was supposed to be here. I may not have brought Rebecca home, but I was able to find her and call out for help."

"I knew God was going to take care of Rebecca," Cheryl said, unable to stop the tears that ran down her cheeks. "But I had no idea it would take all three of you."

"But that's what God does, isn't it? Uses us to help others? If He didn't, we wouldn't need to be here, would we?"

"No, I guess not."

Judith drank the rest of her coffee and then stood up. "I need to get back to the hospital, but before I go, I have something in the car for you."

Cheryl frowned. What could she possibly be talking about?

"If you'll wait here, I'll bring it to you." Judith took her coat off the chair in front of the fireplace. She shrugged it on and smiled. "Nice and dry. Thank you."

"Would you like me to put some coffee in a thermos that you can take with you?" Cheryl asked.

"Oh, honey. That would be wonderful if it's not too much trouble."

Too much trouble? "I think helping to save my daughter's life is worth a little coffee."

"Thank you. I have a feeling I'll be drinking a lot of coffee before that little one arrives."

Judith went out the front door while Cheryl headed to the kitchen. By the time the thermos was ready, Judith was back. She came into the kitchen and put a large plastic bag on the table.

"Pastor Brotton and I sat behind you and your friend at the Honey Bee yesterday. I overheard you tell her about not being able to find a certain doll for Rebecca."

Cheryl, who had just put the thermos on the table next to the bag, was shocked. "You…you found a Baby Plays a Lot?"

Judith nodded. "I found one at an online auction, and then Jordan works with a man who thought his daughter would like one. Turns out she wanted something else. Jordan called him and was able to buy it from him."

So Cheryl had been bidding against Judith? Unbelievable. "But why two…?" She shook her head. "Sari Loudermilk."

"Yes. Pastor Brotton is going to give the doll to her mother— along with some money to help them find their own place near her sister. The church found her a job, so I think she'll get along just fine."

"Is there anyone you haven't helped?"

Judith leaned against the table and sighed. "One. Your friend Timothy. I can help to get rid of the fine he has to pay, but I'm afraid I can't prove he didn't steal all those things. I'm afraid he'll be sent to the county jail. He shouldn't have to spend Christmas there. I don't think he'll be convicted of a crime, but it could take a long time before he's freed."

"My mother-in-law and I have tried so hard to help him. She's the one I was with at the Honey Bee. We know someone is trying to frame him, but we haven't been able to prove it. I'm afraid we're out of time."

Judith was quiet for a moment. "I have a friend in law enforcement who used to tell me, 'Go back to the beginning, where things started to go wrong. Then track things from there.'" She shrugged. "I have no idea if that will help you, but I'm afraid it's all I have."

Cheryl smiled at her. "Thank you. At this point, we have nothing to lose."

After Judith left, Cheryl took the doll and hid it. It would show up under the tree on Christmas morning, proving that Santa hadn't run out of dolls.

Judith's words kept floating through her mind. *Go back to the beginning, where things started to go wrong. Then track things from there.* But what did that mean in this situation? How could she go back to the beginning? To the first theft? She had no idea what that looked like.

She turned off the coffee and cleaned up the kitchen. Then she headed to bed. As she lay there, first she thanked God for taking care of her family. She prayed that He would bless Judith and thanked Him for sending her to Sugarcreek. As she stared up at the ceiling, she prayed that somehow, before Chief Twitchell allowed the county to pick Timothy up, something would happen. Something that would help him.

Go back to the beginning. Go back to the beginning.

Cheryl sat up in bed.

"Are you all right?" Levi mumbled.

"Yes, I'm fine. Don't worry."

He muttered something she couldn't understand and then began to snore again.

Cheryl got out of bed, went into the kitchen, and grabbed her laptop from the small desk Levi had built for her. She opened it and looked up *Timothy Hicks*. She felt something soft rub against her leg and looked down to see Beau watching her.

"If you have any ideas, I could use them now, buddy," she said.

He meowed, sat down, and stared at her.

"I love you too, you silly old cat." She suddenly remembered something she'd intended to do but had forgotten. "Are you trying to remind me?"

He meowed again, and Cheryl laughed. She got up, went to the refrigerator, and took out the container she'd put the rest of the tuna in. Then she put some in Beau's bowl. His tail stayed straight up as he ate, and again his purring filled the room.

Cheryl continued searching the internet for something that might help Timothy. It was a long shot, but at this point, there was nothing else for her to do. Unless someone came forward and admitted that they were behind the thefts and the plan to blame Timothy, he would be thrown into the county jail, where he would stay until they decided whether or not to prosecute him.

She'd only been working about fifteen minutes when she saw something that made her mouth drop open.

She now knew who had been trying to send Timothy back to prison—and why they'd done it.

CHAPTER THIRTY-FIVE

I can't believe you couldn't have found another way to express your grief," Chief Twitchell said to the man sitting across from him.

The chief had allowed Cheryl to sit in on the interview, but he'd cautioned her that she had to be quiet or he'd make her leave.

"It's not fair," the man said. "He took my daughter from me. He doesn't deserve to walk around free. I figured he'd get charged for the burglaries and go back to prison. Anyway, that was my intention." He glared at Chief Twitchell. "I'm not a thief. I didn't keep anything. I left it all in the house where he was staying."

Anger radiated from Terrance Powers, aka Richard Crockett. She felt compassion for him, but his anger was misplaced. At least now Timothy could be exonerated. Judith's advice last night had prompted her to go back to the beginning—the hit-and-run accident that Timothy and his grandfather had been involved in. When she'd looked it up online, she'd discovered an interview with the victim's father. She instantly recognized him and called the chief.

Even though she'd promised she wouldn't interrupt, she had no choice. "Chief Twitchell," she said, "there's something Mr. Powers doesn't know. It's about the accident, and I think it's really important."

The chief frowned at her for a moment but finally nodded. "Go ahead."

Cheryl took a deep breath and prayed that God would help her to get through to the grief-stricken father. She began to tell him what had really happened the night of the accident. At first, she was afraid he wouldn't believe her, but as she repeated what Timothy had told Levi, she could see that there was something about the story that was hitting home with him. When she finished, there was silence in the room. Chief Twitchell had removed his glasses and was wiping his eyes.

"I must admit it bothered me that Timothy never tried to explain what happened," Mr. Powers said slowly. "I overheard him talking to an older man at his sentencing hearing. The man was telling Timothy that he was doing the wrong thing. That he didn't need to go to prison for something he hadn't done. Timothy shut him down. Told him it had to be that way. I assumed he was taking responsibility for killing my daughter because he knew he'd done it."

"That was probably his grandfather," Cheryl said. She paused for a moment, trying to find the right words. "Mr. Powers, I'm so sorry for your loss. I have a daughter. In fact, we almost lost her last night. I can't imagine the pain you've endured. I would never give any credence to Timothy's story unless I really believed it. And I do. I can't tell you what to think, but you must admit that he had a perfect opportunity to blame his grandfather and get himself out of trouble. But he didn't."

Mr. Powers stared at her for a moment. "I don't know. If what you're telling me is the truth, I've made a terrible mistake. Did my grief and my anger overcome my reason?"

"I believe so," Cheryl said. "When Timothy told us what happened that night, he still didn't offer an excuse. I think he really does blame himself for not being more forceful with his grandfather."

"My father refused to stop driving when it was time for him to give up his keys," Mr. Powers said. "Getting him to face the truth took a lot longer than it should have. I was afraid something terrible would happen. Thankfully, it didn't. But if it had, I would have blamed myself."

"It was you who returned the stuffed bear, wasn't it?" Cheryl asked.

He nodded. "I overheard someone at the hotel talking about it—that an older couple had loaned it to your shop. I took it because it was within reach. You have two eagle-eyed clerks who wouldn't take their eyes off your merchandise, but they weren't paying much attention to the Christmas display. When I heard the story about the bear, I felt bad and returned it." He turned his attention to the chief. "So now what?"

"I have to arrest you for stealing," the chief said. "I'm sorry, but I don't have a choice. But I'll speak to the shop owners. If they decide not to press charges, you will be released."

"I have a feeling you'll be going home," Cheryl said with a smile.

"Will you let Timothy go?" Mr. Powers asked.

"Yes. Do you want to speak to him?"

Powers hesitated. "Yes," he said. "I need to ask his forgiveness, and to give him mine."

"I understand," the chief said. "I'm going to let you go back to your hotel and check out and get your things. I'll have one of my officers go with you. While you're gone, I'll release Timothy. You can talk to him after that."

"All right."

The chief stood up and walked out of the room.

"I'm glad you figured it out before I left town," Mr. Powers said.

"Why did you stay around once he'd been arrested?" Cheryl asked.

"Because of the storm. I didn't want to run into it." He sighed.

"How did you find out where Timothy was?"

"I heard he'd come here to meet some old friend. I didn't think he'd be homeless though. That made it harder to find him. That's why I came up with the fake business card and pretended I was a broker. Found a guy on the internet and pretended to be him. It gave me a legitimate reason to ask questions. I didn't know for sure where he was until I talked to you in the restaurant."

"You already had the stolen property. You just needed to find out where to plant it."

"Yes. I planned to add the bear, but, as I said, when I heard it was on loan, I felt bad. I didn't want it kept for evidence with the other things. Besides…" His eyes filled with tears. "It reminded me of a toy my daughter had when she was little." He wiped his eyes. "I'm sorry. I so believed I was doing the right thing. I thought Timothy deserved it. When…when I sat down here with the chief and with you…suddenly everything looked different. I guess I had to face what I'd done. I couldn't twist it around in my mind anymore or tell myself my actions were righteous."

Chief Twitchell came back into his office with Officer Abel following behind him.

"The officer will drive you to your hotel," the chief told Mr. Powers. He looked at Cheryl. "Can you wait here for a minute?"

"Sure."

The chief waited until the two men left the room, then stepped outside the door and gestured at someone. "Okay, bring him in here," he called.

Cheryl could hear footsteps coming down the hallway. When they stopped, Timothy entered the office.

"I'm being released," he said, his voice breaking. "It's…it's over."

"Yes, it is," Cheryl said with a smile.

"The chief told me it was Terrance Powers. He was the one who put those stolen items in the closet."

"Yes, he did. He felt you should spend more time in prison for his daughter's death. I told him what really happened, Timothy. Your grandfather is gone. No one was left to protect."

"No, it's okay. Thank you. Thank you so much. I could never pay you back for—"

Cheryl held up her hand. "You don't owe me anything. Except for one thing."

"Whatever it is, I'll do it if I can."

"Stay with us until you get on your feet, and have Christmas dinner with us."

Timothy blinked several times, and a tear slipped down his cheek. "I can do that," he said. "It sounds great."

Cheryl stood up. "Good. Then let's go home."

Chapter Thirty-Six

Cheryl looked around her kitchen. Not only was this table full, the extra table and chairs that Levi had carried up from the basement were also occupied. Sunday dinner had been incredible. Glazed country ham, au gratin potatoes, sweet potato casserole, two kinds of salad, green beans, corn, and several different kinds of pie, including Naomi's buttermilk pie. Cheryl felt as if she would never eat again. She smiled at Timothy, who sat across from her. His expression gave her joy. If nothing else had come from this Christmas, watching a young man get his life back was more than enough.

Terrance Powers had promised to have the civil suit fine dropped and to return every penny Timothy had already paid. And Judith had spoken to her nephew, Jordan, who helped secure a job for Timothy at the cheese factory after Christmas.

Cheryl reflected on a birth in Bethlehem two thousand years ago that changed the world—and countless lives. The reality of God's love simply overwhelmed her.

"Mama, can I get down?" Rebecca asked. "I want to play with Baby Plays a Lot."

"Yes, you may," Cheryl said. "Wash your hands first."

When Rebecca had opened the package with the doll she'd wanted so badly, she had looked so sad it surprised Cheryl.

"Don't you like it?" Cheryl had asked.

"I love it, Mama. But I think we need to give her to Sari. I don't think she got one. I think this was the last one on Santa's sleigh."

Cheryl's eyes filled with tears as she looked at Levi, who smiled at her.

"I heard that Sari did get a Baby Plays a Lot," Levi said. "So you can keep this one. But I am very proud of you for caring about your friend."

Rebecca's face lit up as she took the doll out of the box and hugged it. Matthew loved his police puppy and wanted to bring it to the table so he could have dinner too, but Levi had persuaded him to leave the toy by the tree. When Rebecca asked to get down from the table, he held up his little arms for someone to pick him up and started asking for his puppy.

"This was a delicious meal," Seth said after Levi got Matthew out of his chair and cleaned up. "And now I think it is only fair that the men clear the table, since the women have spent so much time cooking."

Naomi, Cheryl, Elizabeth, and Esther talked and laughed while the men cleared the table and put the food away. When they returned, Cheryl asked if anyone wanted coffee.

"You stay there for a moment," Levi said. "I will get the coffee. But before that, I have one more gift for you." He headed for their bedroom.

Cheryl frowned at him. He'd given her a beautiful new robe with matching slippers, a pressure cooker, and some books she'd really wanted. Why would he give her anything else?

She looked over at Naomi and could tell that she knew something. "What's going on?"

"I cannot tell you," she said. "But I think it will make you happy."

Levi came back into the kitchen and handed her another box. She opened it carefully and found the king and the lamb from her family's nativity set, looking good as new. Cheryl gasped.

"You can't even tell they were broken. How did you do this?"

"Glue, paint, and a lot of prayer," he said, grinning. Laughter broke out around the table.

"They're perfect. Thank you, honey."

"You're very welcome."

"Now I wish I'd kept the baby Jesus. Maybe you could have fixed that too." Even though she said it, in her heart she knew the piece had been beyond repair.

"Mama, do you really wish you still had baby Jesus?"

Cheryl turned to see Rebecca staring at her from the living room.

"Oh, honey, I don't know. I'm not sure even Daddy could have fixed it."

"But do you want to try, Daddy?" Rebecca asked.

"Ja, I would like to try. Do you know where it is?"

Rebecca nodded. "I didn't want the baby Jesus to go in the garbage, Mama. I got Him out and put Him in the barn. Do you want me to get Him?"

Cheryl looked at Levi. She didn't want Rebecca to be disappointed when she found out that the baby couldn't be glued back together. What should they do?

"Rebecca, get your coat," Levi said. "You and I will go to the barn and get the baby Jesus."

Levi went with her to get her coat on and take her outside.

After they went out the door, Cheryl and Naomi went into the kitchen to get the coffee. Seth and Timothy offered to take care of it, but Cheryl told them they'd done enough. "Cleaning up the dishes and putting the food away means you can rest now," she said with a smile.

As she and Naomi got the coffee maker going and retrieved some mugs, Cheryl said, "So you knew he'd repaired those broken pieces of the nativity?"

Naomi smiled at Cheryl. "Ja. Once they were glued, the cracks still showed. I went to see Barbara Stenzel, who has that craft shop downtown. She told me how to fill in the cracks and then paint the figurines. Levi worked very hard to make them perfect."

"I love that he did that, but I really think the baby is beyond hope. I don't want him or Rebecca to be disappointed."

Naomi shrugged. "We will have to leave it to Gott, ja?"

Cheryl sighed. "Not much else I can do."

She and Naomi had just put the coffee on the table when the front door opened and Levi came in with Rebecca in front of him. Rebecca was carefully holding a paper towel in both hands.

"Matthew is sound asleep on the floor," Levi said quietly. "His arms are around Beau, who is also asleep. We might need to put him to bed soon, but first let us see how much repair this piece needs." He looked down at Rebecca. "Give it to Mama. Let her unwrap it."

"Okay, Daddy." Rebecca carried the paper towel like it was a priceless treasure. She laid it carefully on the table.

"Thank you, honey," Cheryl said. She slowly unwrapped the figurine, not wanting to cause any further damage. When she finally exposed it, she gasped. It wasn't in pieces. It was perfect. As if it had never been damaged.

"Levi, did you do this?" she asked with tears in her eyes. She looked closely at the figurine. There were no cracks or lines anywhere on it.

"No. I did not touch it."

Rebecca's eyes were wide. "Mama, God must have fixed it. Or an angel. Maybe the angel fixed it."

Cheryl and Levi had explained to her more than once that Judith wasn't an angel. And although she nodded when they talked, they were both pretty sure she didn't believe them. To her, Judith was an angel disguised as a human being.

"Maybe she did, sweetheart," Levi said. "Will you put your coat away while I talk to Mama?"

"Yes, Daddy. But it had to be the angel."

"Go on," he said with a smile.

When Rebecca left the room, Levi came over and sat down next to Cheryl. "I knew about the baby. If you had not brought it up, I would have. Now I will tell you what happened, but I must do it quickly before Rebecca returns. When our daughter was lost in the storm and Judith found her, she pulled her inside her coat to keep her warm. Then she began to talk to Rebecca. She believed she should not fall asleep because of the cold. As she forced Rebecca to talk, for some reason Rebecca told Judith about the broken baby. When Judith was at our house, she saw the nativity on the table, with the missing pieces. She contacted me and told me she had the same exact set, but she never used it. She contacted a friend who had a key to her house. The friend went inside, found the set, and retrieved the baby. Then she over-nighted it to our post office, where I picked it up yesterday. We put it back in the barn not only to surprise you but also as a Christmas surprise for Rebecca. We will tell her the real story in a few days, but for now, I think she should enjoy a Christmas miracle."

"It really is a miracle," Esther said. "For a package to reach here in one day...the day before Christmas..."

"She's right," Cheryl said. "We've mailed items for customers at Christmas, and it's taken two weeks for them to reach their destinations."

"I think that is a very good way to look at it," Naomi said. Everyone at the table nodded their agreement."

At that moment, Rebecca came running into the room. She went directly for Cheryl and wrapped her arms around her. Then she stared down at the baby Jesus.

"Mama, the baby Jesus was born in a barn, and this baby was fixed in a barn. That's really neat, isn't it?"

"Yes, Boo. It really is neat."

Rebecca looked up at her. "Mama, this is the best Christmas ever."

Cheryl looked around the table at her family and Timothy, their new friend. "Yes, Rebecca. This is definitely the best Christmas ever."

Cheryl smiled as everyone voiced their agreement. Christmas was about the greatest gift ever given, and today, Cheryl was not only thankful for that gift, but for all the incredible gifts of family and friends she had been given since she moved to Sugarcreek.

There was truly nowhere else in the world she would rather be.

AUTHOR LETTER

Dear Reader,

I was so thrilled to visit my friends in Sugarcreek, Ohio, again. I've missed them. I hope you have enjoyed spending Christmas with Cheryl, Levi, Rebecca, and Matthew, along with their friends, Naomi and Seth Miller.

Not long after the Sugarcreek Amish Mysteries began, I traveled to Sugarcreek and met with my wonderful editor, Susan Downs. I also spent time with the incredible Tricia Goyer. Ever since that special trip, Sugarcreek has stayed in my heart. The town is filled with attractions that will charm you and make you want to stay for days, enjoying the enchantment, simplicity, and beauty of this lovely place. I especially loved their museum, the awesome cheese factory, the world's largest cuckoo clock, and one of my very favorite places in the world, the Honey Bee Café.

I remember sitting inside the Honey Bee, watching cars and buggies drive past the window. The town blends the Amish lifestyle and the modern world beautifully. What a delightful place!

I truly hope you've enjoyed this cozy mystery that includes Christmas and a mysterious angel that seems to pop up in the strangest places!

Merry Christmas from my house to yours!
Or as the Dutch say, *Vrolijk Kerstfeest*!

Blessings,
Nancy Mehl

ABOUT THE AUTHOR

Nancy Mehl lives in Missouri with her husband, Norman, and her very active puggle, Watson. She's authored dozens of books.

All of Nancy's novels have an added touch—something for your spirit as well as your soul. "I welcome the opportunity to share my faith through my writing," Nancy says. "It's a part of me and of everything I think or do. God is number one in my life. I wouldn't be writing at all if I didn't believe that this is what He's called me to do. I hope everyone who reads my books will walk away with the most important message I can give them: God is good, and He loves you more than you can imagine. He has a good plan especially for your life, and there is nothing you can't overcome with His help."

Fun fact about the Amish or Sugarcreek, Ohio

While the Amish do celebrate Christmas, the holiday observation is generally a simpler one, geared more toward family and the religious significance of the holiday than that of most Englischers' celebrations. While there is likely no elaborately decorated Christmas tree in an Amish home, they might decorate with greens and candles. And while their children don't sit on Santa's lap to get their picture taken, they do enjoy making Christmas candies and cookies as a family. The children will often hold a special Christmas program at school as well.

Amish families might exchange small gifts or make handcrafted Christmas cards, and they celebrate Advent on both Christmas Day and the following day, called "second Christmas," which is a time to relax at home or visit friends and relatives. Christmas dinner features a large meal with friends and family gathered around the table, and a worship service, held sometime around the holiday, is an integral part of any Christmas celebration.

Something Delicious from Our Sugarcreek Friends

Amish White Christmas Pie

Ingredients:

1 cup sugar, divided

¼ cup flour

1 envelope unflavored gelatin

½ teaspoon salt

1¾ cup milk

1 teaspoon pure vanilla

¾ teaspoon almond extract

1 cup coconut flakes

3 egg whites

¼ teaspoon cream of tartar

½ cup whipping cream

Baked pie crust

Instructions:

In saucepan, mix ½ cup sugar, flour, gelatin, and salt.

Gradually stir in milk.

Cook over medium heat till boiling.

Boil and stir 1 minute.

Remove from stove and let cool.

Add vanilla, almond extract, and coconut when cool.

Beat egg whites, cream of tartar, and remaining sugar until stiff peaks form. Set aside.

Beat whipping cream until stiff. Set aside.

Transfer cooled mixture into a very large bowl.

Carefully add beaten egg whites and whipped cream. Fold together.

Spoon mixture into baked pie crust.

Sprinkle with coconut and chill for several hours before serving.

Read on for a sneak peek of another exciting book
in the series Sugarcreek Amish Mysteries!

Hark! The Herald Angel Falls
by Tricia Goyer

Cheryl Miller opened the front door and stepped out, noting that the front porch steps needed to be shoveled off yet again. Icy air hit her cheeks, and a shiver ran down her spine. At least another half-inch of snow had fallen in the five hours since Levi had left bright and early. Yet only a few flakes fell now—not enough to stop the community from gathering around the new, life-size nativity scene Levi had built at Community Bible Church, on the corner of Church Street and Main Street near downtown Sugarcreek.

The community had come together to create a live nativity that would last until Christmas Eve, and today's noon celebration officially kicked off the event. Sugarcreek always seemed to come alive during the festivities. With the Swiss architectural styles and the giant cuckoo clock downtown decorated for Christmas, tourists swarmed to the quaint area during the holidays. Adding a drive-by nativity with live characters was yet another way to welcome Christmas shoppers and out-of-towners to the heart of their town.

Today, the community would gather to see church members dressed up as the familiar biblical characters and to enjoy hot cocoa

and cookies. Even though the day proved nippy, the festival celebration was worth it as the people of Sugarcreek and beyond would
be reminded of the true meaning of Christmas.

And I need to be reminded of the true meaning of Christmas,
Cheryl told herself, stepping back inside and shutting the door.
Her life was full of so many wonderful things, yet in the busyness
of the day-to-day, it was easy to forget to slow down, enjoy the
people around her, and remember to turn her heart toward God
and His goodness, no matter what filled her time.

Cheryl was looking forward to things slowing down now that
Levi's big project was finished. After today, she'd have him around
the farm more to help with the kids, which meant she could tackle
the Christmas shopping and baking she'd been putting off.

As head of the live nativity building project, Levi had done his
best to build a sturdy structure and make it comfortable for those
who would participate in the manger scene every evening until
Christmas. Just this morning, as he finished his last sip of coffee,
he told Cheryl he'd tucked a gas-powered heater safely behind the
manger so Mary, Joseph, and any visiting sheep could stay warm.
Of course her thoughtful husband would think of that.

Cheryl glanced at her watch. She and the kids had better get
moving if they were going to make it by noon. She had forty-five
minutes before the nativity program started. She would shovel
the steps, get her kids dressed, and somehow make it to town.
She sighed. She seemed to be running behind on everything
these days.

Soon things will be back to normal.

Cheryl grabbed Levi's jacket by the front door and slipped it on then slid her feet into her snow boots. The jingle of coins and other odd pieces in Levi's pockets caused her to smile. That was one of the things she'd learned about Levi in the years they'd been married. He found every odd bit useful and never threw anything away. "I never know when I'll need something like this," he'd repeat time and again.

As Cheryl prepared to go outside, Rebecca raced up to her. Cheryl smiled at the six-year-old's disheveled hair with curls looping in every direction. Cheryl didn't want to think about her own hair. She knew it was equally a mess. She hadn't run a brush through it since waking up hours ago.

"Thank goodness for hat weather," she mumbled under her breath. Yes, her bright red beanie would come in handy today. Cheryl quickly put it on, tucking her hair inside.

Rebecca tilted her head, curiously eyeing her. "Where are you going?"

Cheryl opened the door, and a swirl of snow rushed in with a blast of wind. "To shovel the steps. It'll take just a minute. And then we're getting in the car for our special outing, remember?"

Rebecca's eyes brightened at the winter wonderland outside the door. "Oh, pretty!"

Cheryl looked down and noticed that Rebecca had only one sock on, and her boots were nowhere in sight. "Your pretty little toes will freeze if you don't finish getting dressed. Didn't I tell you to get some pants and socks on? Oh, and find your coat and boots too. As soon as I clear off this porch we'll be heading out."

"Mommy, look!" Rebecca's squeal pierced the air. Cheryl followed her daughter's gaze to a package on the porch. Airmail labels added a punch of color to the brown box.

"It looks like something from Aunt Mitzi." Cheryl bent down, picked it up, and quickly set it just inside the door. "I'll be right back. Find your boots and coat, okay?"

It took Cheryl no time at all to shovel a pathway down the steps. She would let Levi finish the rest when they returned together that afternoon. He'd get their whole porch and walkway done quickly, and he'd most likely have a smile on his face as he went about his work.

Back inside, Cheryl saw that Rebecca had placed the box on the dining room table.

Rebecca pointed, and her nose crinkled as she smiled. "Aunt Mitzi sent us Christmas presents!"

"You're right. All the way from the other side of the world." Cheryl turned the box to appreciate the variety of postal labels. "Our first Christmas presents this year, delivered right to our doorstep."

Rebecca pointed to the foreign words written in red, in Aunt Mitzi's perfect handwriting, on the side of the box. "What does that say?"

"Well, I actually know this phrase. The last word gives it away. It says '*Bikpela hamamas blong dispela Krismas*,'" Cheryl read, although she was sure she'd mispronounced every word. She smiled, thinking about how her aunt spoke Tok Pisin more often than English in her work in Papua New Guinea. "That means 'Merry Christmas.'"

Rebecca clapped her hands. "Can we open the box?"

"Later, I promise. We're going to go see the live nativity, remember? The angel, Mary, Joseph, and the shepherds will be there. And maybe even sheep. There will be treats for us too." At the mention of the treats, Cheryl paused and looked around. Where was Matthew? Her son was being awfully quiet. If he had been anywhere in earshot, he would have immediately started asking for a treat to take in his pocket for the ride. He asked for one for every car ride, and the napkins on her car's backseat floorboard proved it.

"Matthew's brushing his teeth!" Rebecca exclaimed. Cheryl winced and hurried to the bathroom. She should have been paying closer attention. When had she thought having two kids would be a breeze? Not since the first day they brought Matthew home, that was for sure.

If only I had my act together like Aunt Mitzi, Cheryl scolded herself as she rushed into the bathroom. Three-year-old Matthew smiled at her. His teeth were indeed shiny. Then again, toothpaste covered everything in sight—Matthew's face, the sink, even the tile floor beneath her feet.

Cheryl forced a smile. "Oh Matthew, sweet boy. You're supposed to let Mommy help you, aren't you?"

For the briefest moment, she considered texting Levi and telling him they wouldn't make it to the nativity program today after all, but she knew he would be disappointed. He'd given so much time over the last week to build the set and work with others from the local churches to ensure that everything was perfect. It had been wonderful to see him spending time with new friends, especially when she knew a part of him still felt a little homesick after leaving the Amish.

It took Cheryl a few minutes to get Matthew cleaned up. The bathroom would have to wait. She quickly got him into his jacket and boots. When he was ready, Cheryl was pleasantly surprised to see Rebecca dressed in her boots and coat and standing by the table, eyeing the box from Aunt Mitzi. Beau sat on the table next to the box and fixed his crystal-blue eyes on Cheryl as if he too expected a gift.

Rebecca pointed to the box. "Look, Matthew, Auntie Mitzi sent us presents. Maybe there's one for you or maybe even twooo." She grinned as she drew out the last syllable.

Matthew's eyes widened. "Pwesent for me? Peas?"

Cheryl smiled at her son's toddler speech. "That was nice of you to say *please*." She was about to tell them again that they'd open the box when they got home, but the joy on her children's faces made her give in.

"All right, I'll open the box, but then we have to be on our way. This will only take a minute, right?" she said more to herself than them.

Cheryl found a pair of scissors and cut the tape. A half-dozen small, wrapped packages were nestled inside.

She pulled one out, noting the name. "Rebecca, this present is for you." Even though it was only wrapped in simple brown paper, Rebecca beamed. Cheryl pulled another of equal size out of the box. "And Matthew, here's one for you."

Cheryl pulled a larger package from the box, expecting her name or Levi's. Instead, she saw an unexpected name. *Sarah Miller-Bradley.* Cheryl hadn't seen that name in a while. Not that they hadn't tried to reach out to Levi's sister. As the years had passed, Sarah leaving the Amish to marry an *Englischer* became less of an issue. And then, when Levi had done the same, Cheryl had seen a significant shift in Seth and Naomi, Levi and Sarah's parents. As much as her in-laws still stood by their Amish ways, they maintained a close relationship with her and Levi and the children. Naomi often spoke about how she wanted a closer relationship with Sarah.

How interesting that Aunt Mitzi included a present for Sarah in their box this year.

The clock on the kitchen wall ticked away the time, and Cheryl hurriedly pulled out the next present. This one had the name *Joe* on it, Sarah's husband. The next two gifts had the names she expected on them, *Levi* and *Cheryl.* The final small package had the name *Beau.*

As she lined the presents up on the table, something stirred within Cheryl's heart. She did not doubt that Aunt Mitzi prayed for her, her husband, and her children daily. She also believed that Aunt Mitzi prayed for their extended family too. These gifts demonstrated her love and concern. And now Cheryl had an excellent excuse to reach out to Levi's sister. She smiled at the thought.

"My pwesent!" Matthew said, pointing to his gift.

Beau meowed, as if scolding Matthew for being too loud, and then jumped off the table and sauntered off.

"Yes, and as soon as we get a tree, we'll put these presents under it." Cheryl plopped a knitted cap on her son's head. Then, motioning for Rebecca to follow her to the door, Cheryl scooped Matthew up and put him on her hip. "We'll work on the tree and the presents later, but right now we have to get to town and see the big, big stable your daddy made."

"I want pwesent!" Matthew lunged for the package. Cheryl ignored his efforts, righted him, and hurried to the door.

"We're going to see Daddy and all the sheep and the big nativity set, remember? Daddy's been working so hard on it. We have to hurry. We don't want to be late." Thankfully, the mention of sheep grabbed Matthew's attention.

"Sheep, sheep!" he called as she buckled him into his car seat. When Matthew was secure, Cheryl helped Rebecca buckle hers.

Cheryl tried not to play the comparison game as she drove to town, but it was hard. Aunt Mitzi always seemed to be on top of things. She must have started putting together their Christmas box months ago. Cheryl had yet to purchase one gift for Levi and the children, let alone her extended family. Of course, Naomi would say that things were always a little bit more challenging with little ones underfoot.

"These are the best years of your life." Her mother-in-law's familiar words replayed in Cheryl's mind. And they were true. After so many years of wondering if she'd ever get the family she dreamed of, Cheryl had to remind herself that she had all she'd prayed for, and they were named Rebecca, Matthew, and Levi.

Cheryl hummed a Christmas carol as she drove, choosing to keep a happy attitude and a thankful heart, despite the strain of the past week. Before she'd married Levi, she'd been drawn to his caring nature, giving attitude, and strong work ethic. She wouldn't fault him for that now.

Fifteen minutes later, Cheryl had parked the car and gotten the kids out of their car seats. She smiled to herself, amazed that she'd gotten to the event on time. It was only when she adjusted her scarf that she realized she was wearing Levi's coat instead of her own. She had put it on to shovel the walk and must have grabbed it and thrown it on without thinking when she'd rushed out the door with the kids. She must look a fright. Oh well. She'd fit right in with the shepherds and their sheep.

The ring of a hammer echoed in the air as Cheryl approached the front lawn of Community Bible Church.

"Daddy! I see him!" Rebecca bounced at Cheryl's side, squeezing her gloved hand tighter.

Cheryl paused, looking up at the barnlike structure. Sure enough, Levi was hammering up a piece of the stable that must have fallen off. Cheryl released a low whistle. It looked like there were over a hundred people in the crowd standing on the lawn between the parking lot and the nativity set.

Just as Levi finished and slipped his hammer into his tool belt loop, the bleating of an escaped sheep caught his attention. He immediately took off after it. A fully dressed wise man joined the chase. Laughter from the crowd moved in a wave across the lawn as more people caught sight of the mishap.

Rebecca tugged on Cheryl's hand, pulling in the direction of the crowd. "Can we go see Daddy?"

"Not yet, Boo. It looks like he's busy helping one of the wise men round up that stray sheep."

Rebecca bounced on her toes, her boots making a squeaky sound on the snow. "Is that barn going to stay at the church always?"

"It does look like a barn, doesn't it? It's a nativity set, just like the little one we have at home."

Rebecca's eyes widened. "That's going to have to be a big baby Jesus."

Cheryl laughed. "It's going to be a pretty big baby doll. But it'll be more like one of the dollies you play with, not a ceramic one like in our nativity set."

Rebecca didn't respond to Cheryl's comment about the doll, and Cheryl knew her daughter's mind had already moved on to other things, likely the huge red ornaments that hung in the pine tree just to the left of the nativity set and the long table laden with steaming hot cocoa and cookies next to the tree. Sure enough, Rebecca began to pull in that direction, and Cheryl followed with Matthew in tow.

Cheryl's eyes widened when she noticed a familiar person standing near the cookie display. She gasped. "It can't be," she said to herself. After all these years. *How in the world did Aunt Mitzi know?*

A Note from the Editors

We hope you enjoyed another exciting volume in the Sugarcreek Amish Mysteries series, published by Guideposts. For over seventy-five years, Guideposts, a nonprofit organization, has been driven by a vision of a world filled with hope. We aspire to be the voice of a trusted friend, a friend who makes you feel more hopeful and connected.

By making a purchase from Guideposts, you join our community in touching millions of lives, inspiring them to believe that all things are possible through faith, hope, and prayer. Your continued support allows us to provide uplifting resources to those in need. Whether through our online communities, websites, apps, or publications, we strive to inspire our audiences, bring them together, and comfort, uplift, entertain, and guide them. Visit us at guideposts.org to learn more.

We would love to hear from you. Write us at Guideposts, P.O. Box 5815, Harlan, Iowa 51593 or call us at (800) 932-2145. Did you love *When Angels Whisper*? Leave a review for this product on guideposts.org/shop. Your feedback helps others in our community find relevant products.

Find inspiration, find faith, find Guideposts.

Shop our best sellers and favorites at
guideposts.org/shop
Or scan the QR code to go directly to our Shop

Find more inspiring stories in these best-loved Guideposts fiction series!

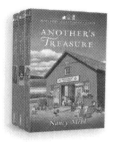

Mysteries of Lancaster County

Follow the Classen sisters as they unravel clues and uncover hidden secrets in Mysteries of Lancaster County. As you get to know these women and their friends, you'll see how God brings each of them together for a fresh start in life.

Secrets of Wayfarers Inn

Retired schoolteachers find themselves owners of an old warehouse-turned-inn that is filled with hidden passages, buried secrets, and stunning surprises that will set them on a course to puzzling mysteries from the Underground Railroad.

Tearoom Mysteries Series

Mix one stately Victorian home, a charming lakeside town in Maine, and two adventurous cousins with a passion for tea and hospitality. Add a large scoop of intriguing mystery, and sprinkle generously with faith, family, and friends, and you have the recipe for *Tearoom Mysteries*.

Ordinary Women of the Bible

Richly imagined stories—based on facts from the Bible—have all the plot twists and suspense of a great mystery, while bringing you fascinating insights on what it was like to be a woman living in the ancient world.

To learn more about these books, visit Guideposts.org/Shop